DON'T LOOK BACK IN MANGER

IAN EDWARDS

PAUL WALLER

DISCLAIMER

This is a work of fiction. Names, characters, businesses, places events and incidents are products of the author's imagination. Any resemblance to actual persons, living or dead or actual events is purely coincidental.

This book is dedicated to everyone who has bought our books and provided such a positive response. We hope you enjoy this as much as we enjoyed writing it.

HAPPY CHRISTMAS

ACKNOWLEDGMENTS

We would like to again thank Fareeha Durrani for her enthusiasm and invaluable assistance in the development of this novel.

A big thank you to Mike Mason for a fantastic cover.

LEAVE A REVIEW

We hope you enjoy this book - if you did we would really appreciate it you could leave a short review.

Reviews really make a difference for the authors and help the books attract a wider audience.

You can can rate this book or leave a short review here:

Amazon.com
Amazon.co.uk
Goodreads.

Alternatively you wish to contact us directly through our website at edwardswaller.com

YOU WILL BE READING ABOUT

~~You have been watching~~

Alan Rose - Gave up a career in the civil service to become a full time comedian but now lacks motivation. For the previous eighteen months he has been haunted by the ghost of Frankie Fortune.

Frankie Fortune - A minor music hall celebrity making a comeback on the alternative comedy scene of the 1980s before his untimely death. Now spends his time haunting Alan. He can only be seen and heard by Alan.

Sarah Gayle - Divides her time between running the local arts centre and managing Alan and Harry.

Harry Hodges - After retirement turned his appalling ventriloquist act into a stand up routine.

James Cook - Alan's best friend. The only person that Alan has told about Frankie.

Rosie Talbot - Alan's girlfriend.

Amy Cook - James's wife and primary school teacher. (Both roles are equally as challenging) .

ONE

'So, I'm looking at this great big box...' Alan held his hands four feet apart. 'It's massive. Clearly the biggest present under the tree, all wrapped up in tacky cheap Christmas paper, covered in Father Christmases and sleighs. He let the enormity of this sink in. 'And then,' Alan continued. 'I hear my mum say, *"Aren't you going to open it?"* So, I tear off the paper in a frenzy. There's non-recyclable shiny wrapping paper all over the place and I'm really excited. And finally, there it is...A leaf blower.'

Someone laughed.

'I was fourteen.'

A few more giggles.

'I can assure you that at no point in the lead-up to Christmas...actually at no point in my previous fourteen years had I ever said to my parents; *"forget the BMX or the football kit. What I really want is a leaf blower."'*

A burst of laughter cut through the faint mumbling.

Alan laughed as though he had thought of this for the first time. 'I suppose it was my parents' way of getting me to help out in the garden. I imagine my mum said to my dad,

"*Buy him a practical present.*" To be honest, I would have sooner had an angle grinder...That would have taught Pythagoras to keep his theories to himself.'

He looked down at the audience. On the table nearest to him, someone nudged the waiter's arm and a Brussel sprout fell from a serving spoon into a glass of wine, receiving the biggest laugh of the night. Alan sighed as a little piece of him died inside.

TWO WEEKS EARLIER

Alan studied the sheet of paper in front of him. 'No, no, definitely not. No, no...I don't think so. Not that one either. I've been there. It's bloody awful.' He handed the sheet of paper across the desk to Sarah. 'Nothing there I fancy.'

'I'm sorry, Alan,' Sarah snatched the paper back. 'You appear to be a little confused.'

Alan raised an eyebrow. 'I am?'

'Yes. You appear to have misunderstood how this works. I am your manager and your agent, and it is, believe it or not, my job to find you work.' Sarah smiled. 'Not to provide you with a list of venues that you may or may not grant with your presence.'

'Eh?'

'We've had this conversation on numerous occasions. You're supposed to be a comedian. So, get out there and do some comedianing or give it up.'

Alan frowned. 'Comedianing? Is that a real word?'

Sarah glared at him.

'All I'm saying is that there's nothing in this,' Alan tapped the sheet of paper. 'That really gets me excited.'

'Well, if you don't fancy it, I'll have no problem finding someone who does want the work,' Sarah huffed.

Alan groaned and reached out for the paper, quickly re-scanning the list. 'How about this one? The Apollo Hotel. What's happening there?'

'Christmas themed evening. Three course meal, two comedians and finishing with a disco.'

'Two comedians?'

'I already booked Harry for it.'

Alan nodded and sighed. 'OK, I'll do it. Where is it?'

'It's a large hotel, part of a chain, in Hammersmith.' Sarah picked up her phone, scrolling through the menu. 'I have the email here. There are two groups booked in: The local atheists and a firm of management consultants.'

'Management consultants,' Alan pulled a face. 'I hate management consultants. They're like civil servants, but they get ten times the salary by doing ten times less work.'

'Well, try not to upset them.'

Alan grinned. 'I'll do my best.'

Alan walked off stage to where Harry stood waiting in the wings, idly picking bits of fluff from Old Man Ernie's suit jacket. The dummy was perched on a stool wearing a scaled-down version of the same beige suit Harry was wearing.

'Don't you hate it when that happens?' Alan asked.

Harry looked up. 'What's that?'

'When you turn up to a swanky hotel gig and someone's wearing the same thing as you.'

Harry laughed. 'It was Katherine's idea. She thought we'd look more like a double act.'

Alan stared at his friend and the ventriloquist dummy and shook his head. 'Go on then. Off you go.'

Harry straightened the dummies tie and picked him up. 'See you later,' he said and hurried past Alan and onto the stage.

———

Frankie Fortune stood at the back of the room watching Harry, deep in conversation with Old Man Ernie. The crowd, those sober enough to pay attention, were split over Harry's routine. Some found his deliberate mistakes hilarious, while others stared in disbelief as Harry made no attempt to hide his moving lips while attempting to straighten his false moustache.

Frankie laughed out loud as Harry's attempt to perform a card trick sent the pack of cards over the nearest table. Someone shouted *"You're rubbish"* from one of the tables, clearly missing the joke. Harry had spent the last year perfecting his 'disastrous' act. It was so well choreographed that, to the untrained eye, Harry didn't appear to have a clue what he was doing. Frankie watched Harry's chaotic attempt to clear the cards up and then went off to find Alan.

———

Frankie found Alan in the corner of the adjoining bar, idly swiping through his phone.

'It's like Santa's Grotto in here,' Frankie said, gesturing round around the room.

Alan looked up from his phone. Tinsel and streamers hung from the ceiling. Each table had a festive centrepiece and an eight-foot Christmas tree stood in the middle of the room. Alan held his phone as if he were on a call. This simple solution stopped on-lookers wondering why he was talking to himself. 'They might have overdone it a bit...' He said.

'How did it go tonight?' Frankie asked.

Alan sighed. 'The sprouts got a bigger laugh.'

'Tough crowd?'

'Not for the vegetables.'

'It doesn't sound any better for Harry. I haven't heard much laughter from next door.'

Alan looked around the bar. It was empty save for a couple deep in conversation. 'It's the crowd. They don't want to be entertained anymore. It's all self-promotion, taking photographs of themselves at the gig rather than experiencing it. They've no interest in being entertained. Their entertainment is trying to get a bigger laugh through heckling.'

'Bloody hell, son, you sound really pissed off. Trust me, it's always been the same. In my day, I used a few put-downs that I'd roll out when needed.' Frankie smiled. 'I remember one time I called someone out and told him to sit back in the chair while I plugged it in. It didn't go down too well.'

'Why?' Alan asked.

'It was the Royal Variety Performance.'

Harry scooped Old Man Ernie from the stool and hurried off the stage as a mince pie flew past his shoulder and hit the wall behind him, breaking into several sticky pieces. He turned to face the diners. 'I only said...' A roast potato hit him squarely in the chest, getting the biggest cheer of the night.

Another potato struck Old Man Ernie on the head, knocking his paper crown off.

The hotel's events manager, Ivor Fulsack, hurried past him onto the stage as Harry disappeared out of sight. He gave Harry a reproachful look and shook his head.

'Ladies and Gentlemen,' Mr Fulsack spoke into the mic. 'I don't think it's necessary to express your dissatisfaction with tonight's comedians in such an aggressive manner,' he said as a ball of stuffing hit him on the head.

'I mean, what kind of atheists have a Christmas party?' Alan drained his bottle of beer. 'Are they progressives?'

'Maybe they're just really bad atheists?' Frankie added. 'They're prepared to put their beliefs aside at Christmas to have a jolly-up.'

The sound of cheering emanated from the function room next door.

'Sounds like Harry has finally broken through,' Alan said, while trying to attract the barman's attention.

'Or broken out.'

Alan pulled a face. 'What?'

Frankie gestured at the door. 'He's just walked in.'

Harry waved from the doorway and made his way over.

'How did it go?' Alan asked, waving frantically at the barman.

Harry sat Old Man Ernie on a chair. 'A bloody nightmare. An absolute bloody nightmare.' He dropped into the remaining chair with a sigh.

Alan, having no luck catching the barman's eye, held two fingers up. 'That good?' He asked, turning back to

Harry, who was busy brushing bits of Christmas pudding from his jacket.

'I sometimes wonder why we bother.'

'Tell me about it,' Alan gestured at one of the empty bottles on the table in front of him. 'Want one?' He asked.

Harry nodded, and Alan stood up. 'I'll be back.'

Alan wandered up to the bar, ordered two bottles of beer, and held his bank card against the card reader.

'Is that a child?'

Alan frowned. 'Who?'

The barman leaned forward. 'Over there, sitting at your table.'

Alan slipped his card back into his pocket. 'No children at our table, just three very pissed off comedians.'

It was the barman's turn to frown. 'Three? Child comedian, is he?'

Realising his error, Alan reached for his beers.

The barman continued. 'No children in this bar. He'll have to go outside.'

'There are no children at my table...' Alan looked around the room. 'There are no children in here. In fact, there's no one else here. Your bar is empty. Just two very fed up and thirsty comedians.'

'The kid can't stay,' the barman repeated. 'We have a very strict code.'

'For crying out loud,' Alan snapped. 'I've told you there are no children in here.' He turned around and gestured around the room. 'Look...' He paused. Sitting at the table between Harry and Frankie with his back to the bar was Old Man Ernie. 'Do you mean that child?' He pointed at the dummy.

The barman leaned across the bar. 'Yes, him. He's not allowed in here. He can wait outside until you've finished.'

Alan smiled. 'He's not a child.'

The barman retreated to his side of the bar. 'He looks like a child.'

'No, he's a d...'

'Dwarf?' The barman interrupted.

'No, he's a dummy. A ventriloquist's dummy.'

'Is he?' The barman leaned across the bar for a better look.

Alan sighed. 'Come with me,' he said, setting off back to the table.

The barman hesitated, looked around the empty bar, decided there was unlikely to be a rush on in the next minute or so, and followed Alan.

Frankie and Harry looked up as Alan approached the table.

'Harry, can you show Mr Barman here Old Man Ernie?'

Harry looked from Alan to the barman. 'Sorry?'

Alan grabbed hold of the barman's arm and pulled him round the table. 'Look.'

Old Man Ernie grinned manically back at them.

'Does he look like a child to you?' Alan knocked on his head. 'See...wood.'

The barman chewed his lip. 'I suppose so.'

'Alan,' Harry said. 'What's going on?'

'Mr Barman here thought Ernie was a child.'

The barman nodded. He reached out and prodded the dummy in the chest. 'OK...He can stay.'

TWO

'...It's only eight sleeps to the big day...come on guys, admit it. You're not ready, are you?'

A hand shot out from under the duvet, banged the top of the clock radio several times in an unsuccessful attempt to turn the volume down before giving up and pushing it off the bedside table with a crash. He heard footsteps noisily climbing the stairs and pulled the duvet further over his head.

'What happened?' Rosie asked breathlessly. 'Are you OK? I heard a crash and ...' She paused, noticing the clock radio on the floor. 'Why is the radio on the floor?'

'It fell off,' Alan mumbled from under the duvet.

'Things do not fall off other things unless they've been pushed. I thought you'd had a fall.'

Alan wriggled his top half free from the duvet and propped himself up on his elbows. 'What do you mean *had a fall*? I'm not old. You don't start having falls until you're at least sixty.'

Rosie folded her arms and leaned against the wall. 'OK, I thought you had fallen over. Happy now?'

Alan grunted something unintelligible, put his head back on the pillow and stared at the ceiling.

'Anyway, why is the radio on the floor?'

'That idiot,' he gestured in the general direction of the radio. 'Going on about so many sleeps until Christmas. His only job is to tell us the news, maybe provide some insightful editorial comment. Instead, he's wittering on like a nursery schoolteacher.'

'Insightful editorial comment,' Rosie repeated. 'You're listening to *Superstar Steve's Sensational Breakfast Show*. This is as good as it gets.'

'The man's a fool. The radio had to go.'

Rosie sighed. 'Why do you have to be so loud?' Can't you just turn the radio off like a normal person? Why does everything have to be so noisy with you?'

'It's not,' Alan grumbled, slipping back under the duvet. 'Anyway, it's too early.'

Rosie shook her head. 'It's nine thirty. Normal people are already up and doing stuff.'

Alan's head emerged from the duvet again. 'Why are you still here? Shouldn't you be at work?'

'I told you, I have today off. I'm going Christmas shopping with Jayne.'

'Oh yeah, I remember,' Alan lied.

'You could come with us?'

'I'd love to.' Another lie. 'But I've got a lot on today. I'm rushed off my feet.'

'Clearly,' Rosie shook her head, told him to put the radio back where it belonged, and left the bedroom. Alan listened to her footsteps descending the stairs, buried his head under the pillow and fell back to sleep.

When Alan eventually woke up, he was fairly sure Rosie had left for the day. He padded across the bedroom and waited at the door, listening for any noise. He didn't fancy walking into the kitchen and finding Rosie and Jayne having a pre-shopping coffee and passing judgment on his Batman boxer shorts.

'What are you doing?'

Alan jumped, startled by the voice in his ear. 'What the...'

'What's the matter?' Frankie Fortune asked.

Alan looked at the late middle-aged man standing in front of him, dressed in his usual bottle green velvet evening jacket over a frilly shirt and bow tie. 'Do you have to do that?'

'Do what?'

'Popping up next to me? Haunting me? It's off-putting.'

Frankie shoved his hands in his pockets, looked over the landing and down the stairs. 'I'm a ghost. That's what I do. If you like, I'll try to rustle up some chains or do some wailing before I get here? Give you a bit of notice.'

'Yeah, that'll do. Or you could just stop coming round.'

Ignoring him, Frankie asked again. 'What are you doing standing around in your pants?'

Alan sighed. 'I'm checking to see whether Rosie has left. She's going Christmas shopping with her sister.'

Frankie slipped past him and made his way down the stairs, complaining all the while about his dodgy feet. On reaching the kitchen, he called back. 'It's clear.'

Alan went back into the bedroom, pulled on an old sweatshirt, and joined Frankie in the kitchen.

'What happened to you last night?' Alan asked while making himself a cup of tea and pouring cereal into a bowl. 'I looked round, and you'd gone.'

'You and Harry seemed to be having a good time, so I thought I'd leave you to it.'

Alan laughed. 'It was a good night...Once I'd got the gig out of the way.' He took a mouthful of tea. 'I'll say this about the atheists. They really know how to party.'

'Are you ringing?' Frankie asked, looking around the kitchen.

Alan looked at him, mumbling something unintelligible through a mouthful of cereal.

'Is that your phone ringing?' Frankie repeated.

Alan stopped chewing and listened. 'Sounds like it. Unless someone's playing a xylophone in a cupboard.'

He stood up, patting his sweatshirt and pants. 'Where's my phone?' He asked, opening a cupboard.

'It's coming from out there,' Frankie nodded at the open door.

Alan strode past Frankie into the hallway, before stopping at the foot of the stairs. The noise was louder but muffled. 'Where is it?'

'Found it?' Frankie asked.

'No. I think it must be...It's stopped.'

'Can't be important then,' Frankie called back.

'Exactly,' Alan agreed. 'If it were important, they'll ring back.'

The noise began again. A muffled xylophone.

'I guess it is important,' Frankie said. 'You'd better answer it before it gets annoying.'

Alan huffed and held his hands up. 'I don't know where it is, do I?' He paused for a moment, adding, 'And it *is* getting annoying.'

Frankie frowned, wandering from the kitchen. 'If I didn't know better, I'd say it was coming from upstairs.'

'Are you sure?' Alan took a step towards the living room. 'I thought it was coming from in here.'

'Go on, then.' Frankie ushered him towards the door. 'It's getting on my nerves now.'

Alan stepped over one of his discarded shoes on his way back into the living room. 'Actually, I think it's quieter in here.'

'I told you,' Frankie said. 'It's coming from upstairs. Oh, it's stopped again.'

Alan shrugged. 'It can't be that important if they keep hanging up. It's probably someone dicking around. I'm going to finish my breakfast.'

As he moved back towards the kitchen, the xylophone started again.

'For crying out loud,' Frankie cried out.

'I think it's coming from below,' Alan said, looking down.

'Has the house got a cellar?' Frankie asked.

Alan shook his head. 'I don't know, Rosie never said.'

'Haven't you ever asked?' Frankie frowned. 'It could be a locked room Rosie keeps hidden from you.'

'Well, there is the one she keeps the deformed relatives locked in.'

Alan looked down then up at Frankie, who returned Alan's grin. 'Obviously,' they said in unison. Alan reached down, picked up his shoe and pulled his phone out. 'It's Harry.' He swiped across the screen. 'Harry.'

'Hello, Alan.' Harry said. 'I hope I didn't wake you?'

'No, no. I had to get up anyway. My phone was ringing.' Frankie smirked.

'Oh, that's OK then,' Harry said. 'Listen, Alan, something terrible has happened.'

'What's up?'

'Old Man Ernie has gone.'

'Gone? What do you mean gone? He's a dummy. He's not going to pack his bags and run off with the garden gnome next door.' Alan looked at Frankie and mouthed. 'He's lost it.'

'He's not here. I've looked everywhere. He's not even in his favourite chair.'

'Sorry, did you just say his favourite chair?'

'Ernie likes to sit in the armchair nearest the TV.'

'Are you still drunk?'

On the other end of the line, Harry sighed. 'Seriously Alan, he's not here. I've looked everywhere...I'm really worried.'

'When did you last see him?' Alan asked, trying not to laugh.

'I can't remember. I think he was in the bar with us, but it's all a bit hazy.'

Alan thought back to the previous night. 'He was definitely in the bar, but you're right, it's a bit of a blur. You'd better come over and we'll try to piece the night together.'

'OK. Thanks Alan,' Harry replied. 'I'll see you in a bit.'

'What was that all about?' Frankie asked as Alan ended the call.

Alan slipped back behind the table, prodded his now stodgy cereal with his spoon before pushing it to one side. 'Harry thinks Old Man Ernie has run away. He can't find him.'

'Nothing to do with you both being blind drunk last night?' Frankie pointed out.

'He's conveniently overlooking that at the moment.'

'Shouldn't you be getting changed?' Frankie said.

'Harry has suffered enough losing Old Man Ernie, without seeing you in your boxer shorts.

'No need.'

'Why?'

'Because in about five minutes he'll call me back and tell me he's found Ernie in the fridge or something.'

'The fridge?'

'You always end up putting things in funny places when you're drunk. Ben down the pub thinks that's why he's got four kids. Trust me, in about five minutes he'll be calling me.'

'Really?'

Alan leaned back in his chair, hands behind his head. 'Have faith.'

ONE HOUR LATER

'Why are you wearing boxer shorts?' Harry asked as Alan opened the door.

'It's a fashion statement,' Alan shut the door.

'Oh, OK,' Harry mumbled and wandered through to the kitchen.

'You didn't find him then?' Alan asked.

Harry shook his head. 'No, I looked everywhere.'

'Did you check the fridge?'

'Sorry, why would I check the fridge?'

Alan sighed. 'I think the question you need to ask is why didn't I look in the fridge? When I've had a few, I often find things in unusual places. I once found my shoes in the bin after a heavy night.'

Harry frowned. 'I got some milk out of the fridge this morning and I didn't see him in there.'

'OK,' Alan nodded. 'Sounds like he's gone, then.'

'Did Harry actually take him home with him?' Frankie asked. 'When I left, you were both pretty drunk.'

'Harry,' Alan said. 'Can you remember taking Ernie home? Actually...' Alan paused. 'How did you get home? I can't remember you leaving. Actually, I can't remember leaving myself.'

Frankie shook his head and groaned.

'Cab,' Harry announced. 'I seem to remember getting into a cab.'

'Yes, but did you have Ernie with you?'

'Yes. Definitely...I think...Probably.'

Alan sighed. 'Great. That's really helpful.'

Harry sat at the table and stared at Alan's congealed cereal. 'What's this?'

'My breakfast. Or at least it would have been if someone hadn't lost their co-star.' He turned to the kettle. 'Tea?'

Harry nodded. 'Please.'

'When's your next gig?' Alan asked.

'End of the week,' Harry said gloomily. 'What am I going to do without him?'

Alan chewed his lip. 'Can you use that other dummy you've got? Timmy or Tommy? The kid one.'

Harry shook his head. 'No, it wouldn't be right. It would be like Morecambe without Wise.'

'Flanagan without Allen,' Frankie said.

'The Two Ronnies,' Alan added. 'Without err...one of them.'

'I'm going to have to tell Sarah,' Harry announced. 'If I can't do my next gig, she'll have to book someone else.'

'I'll come with you,' Alan told him.

'Thanks,' Harry said. 'One thing though.'

'What's that?'

'Can you put some trousers on?'

THREE

Sarah sat at her desk, comparing the figures on her laptop to those on the sheet of paper in front of her. She drew a line through across the paper with a yellow highlighter pen and sighed. Ticket sales for the pantomime were disappointing. She needed a concerted effort to push sales in the next few days if the event wasn't to end in yet another disaster. She grew more disillusioned with her job at the local Arts Council with each passing day. Every event was either a financial black hole or beset with increasingly bizarre mishaps.

Not for the first time, Sarah thought about handing in her notice. Juggling her day job with her role as agent and manager for several comedians was taking its toll on her wellbeing. Something had to give. Her frustration at work mirrored her frustration with Alan. If he took comedy more seriously, she felt he could really go places. And as his manager, she could travel with him. But his inertia was wearing her down. She exhaled loudly, refocusing on the task at hand.

'Perhaps,' she said to herself. 'The idea of using an

actual wolf for the production of *Little Red Riding Hood* had put people off.'

She scratched her head. They had signed all the necessary health and safety paperwork and the wolf would be chained at all times. Plus, a zookeeper was on standby with a tranquilizer gun. Sarah couldn't believe it wasn't more popular.

Voices and movement outside her door caused Sarah to tear her eyes from her work.

'Hello?' she called out.

Alan poked his head round the door and grinned. 'Alright.'

'Why are you skulking around outside?' She asked.

'We're not skulking.' Alan sat down with a huff.

'We?'

'Yeah, me and Harry. He's outside talking to your receptionist.'

'Sally?'

Alan nodded. 'When Harry met Sally.'

With perfect timing, Harry wandered into the office, dragged a chair across the floor and sat next to Alan. 'Morning Sarah,' he said.

'It's Captain Chaos and the boy no-show. Sarah mocked.

'Sorry?' Alan looked at Harry, who shrugged in response.

'I'm glad you popped in this morning,' Sarah began. 'I had a call this morning from the manager of the hotel you were at last night. They said you...' She looked at Alan. 'Were fifteen minutes late and then offered an abridged version of your routine which lasted all of...' She pulled a post it note from the edge of her screen. 'Another fifteen minutes, while you...' She glared at Harry, who smiled back at her. 'Upset everyone in the audience to the extent they threw food at you.'

'Oh, come on,' Alan protested. 'The crowd was rubbish. They had no interest in us at all. All they wanted to do was get pissed and give us a hard time.'

'And throw food,' Harry added. 'It's true. I could have been seriously injured if one of those Christmas puddings had a sixpence in it.'

Alan leaned closer. 'In fact, he's thinking of suing. You can tell the manager that the next time he phones to complain.'

Sarah laughed. 'He said you were in the bar until it closed.'

'We had a few Christmas drinks with some guests,' Harry explained.

'A few? I'm told it was more than a few. The only reason the hotel will have you back is because you spent more in the bar afterwards than they paid you for the night.'

'So, I earned nothing last night?' Alan asked.

Sarah shook her head. 'You spent every penny you earned, and then some.'

Alan rubbed his head. 'I suppose that would explain the headache.'

Harry shook his head. 'I told him to slow down,' he told Sarah.

'Perhaps you should have taken your own advice,' Sarah pointed out. 'Because you did the same. In fact, the manager wanted me to thank you on his behalf after you...' She pulled another post-it note from her desk. 'And these are his words, *"offered to buy the bar a drink"*. How drunk did you both get?'

Alan shrugged. Harry looked down at his shoes before saying, 'We were in the Christmas spirit.'

'I don't care,' Sarah laughed. 'You spend your money where you want.'

Sarah turned back to her PC and began tapping away at the keyboard.

'Harry has something to tell you,' Alan said.

'What's that, Harry?' She asked, still tapping away at the keys.

'I can't find Old Man Ernie.'

Sarah stopped tapping. 'What do you mean?'

Harry shuffled his chair closer to the desk. 'I can't find him. I've looked everywhere.'

Sarah looked at Alan, who shrugged helplessly.

'Sorry Harry,' Sarah said. 'I don't have him.'

'Well, you see, the problem is, I have a gig on Friday, and I can't do it without Ernie. We're a double act.'

Sarah sighed, turning her attention to Alan. 'Can't you help him?'

'No chance. I'm not sitting on his lap, and I don't want to find out where he puts his hand.'

'I mean!' Sarah snapped before taking a deep breath and continuing. 'Can you help him find Ernie?'

'I did.'

'You did?'

'Did you?' Harry asked.

Alan sighed. 'I told him to look all over his house.'

'That's not really helping, is it?' Sarah waited for a response. When none was forthcoming, she continued. 'I was thinking of actual physical help.'

Alan shrugged. 'Harry has already looked all over his house.'

'Twice,' Harry added.

'How did you get home?' Sarah asked Harry.

'Alan called me a cab.'

'Have you spoken to the cab company? You may have left Ernie in the cab.'

Alan nodded. 'Brilliant. Why didn't we think of that?' He dug his phone out of his pocket, scrolling through his list of calls. 'There you go,' he passed the phone to Harry. 'It's the number at the top.'

Harry tapped the screen and held the phone to his ear. 'It's ringing,' he told them.

'Any chance of a coffee?' Alan whispered to Sarah, who huffed and made a show of pushing her chair back and standing up.

'Chocolate biscuits would be nice too, he added, receiving a glare from Sarah before she left the office.

'What?'

'Shush.' Harry hissed and pointed to the phone in his hand.

'Hello,' Harry said into the phone. 'I wonder if you can help me?... No, I don't want to go anywhere. I went somewhere yesterday. Well, actually it was today, earlier this morning...'

He looked at Alan and shook his head. 'I *am* trying to get to the point, but you keep interrupting me. OK, thank you.' He took a deep breath. 'At about three o'clock this morning, one of your cabs took me from the Apollo Hotel in Hammersmith to my home in Fulham. I think I... No, I don't know his name... I can't remember. Hang on, I'll check.' He put his hand over the phone and turned to Alan. 'What make of car was it?'

Alan shrugged. 'No idea. I think it was silver.'

'I think it was silver,' Harry repeated. 'I know silver isn't a make of car. No, I doubt I'd recognise the driver. I only saw the back of his head. What? Dark and curly, I think... I told you, I don't know his name, but if you tell me, it's

Abdul, then I'm happy to accept it was him...No, I wasn't sick in the back of his car...I think I'd remember that... As far as I can recall the car did not smell of sick either, so I would assume whoever was sick in the back of Abdul's car was picked up after me... Well, that's good. Can you ask Abdul if he found a ventriloquist's dummy in the back of his cab this morning? I appear to have lost mine... OK, thank you.'

Any joy?' Alan asked.

'He's gone to ask Abdul.'

Alan nodded. 'That's something then.'

'Hello...' Harry said, resuming the call. 'Well, he's about three feet tall and he was wearing...Hang on. How many lost ventriloquist dummies have you found?... What do you mean *standard lost property procedure*?... No, I'm not trying to be funny...'

'Trust me, he's definitely not,' Alan sniggered.

'Yes, of course I want him back...OK, sorry...He's about three feet tall, straight brown hair and he's wearing a brown suit, white shirt and a brown tie. His name's Ernie... So do you have him?'

Sarah stepped into the room holding a tray on which rested three mugs and a packet of biscuits. 'Any joy?' She asked as she placed the tray on the desk.

'Not sure,' Alan told her. But it sounds promising.'

'What do you mean, you haven't got him?' Harry barked into the phone. 'I've just described him to you...Yes, of course. Standard lost property procedure...If I give you my number, could you call me if he turns up? ... Hello, hello...'

Harry passed the phone back to Alan. 'He's hung up.'

'I assume they haven't got him?' Sarah asked.

Harry shook his head. 'No.'

Alan reached across the desk for a mug. 'So, if he's not

at home, and you haven't left him in the cab, there's only one place he can be.'

Harry groaned. 'Does this mean I have to go back to the hotel?'

'Don't worry,' Sarah said. 'Alan will go with you.'

'Will I?'

'Yes.'

Alan slumped back into his chair, dunking a chocolate biscuit into his coffee. He mumbled something under his breath.

'Are you still here?' Sarah asked, waving them on their way.

FOUR

'I've been thinking,' Harry said as he and Alan walked from Hammersmith underground station towards the hotel.

'You remembered where you left Ernie?' Alan asked.

'No. I haven't a clue what I did with him. It's something else. I was thinking this might be a sign.'

'A sign?'

'Yes. A sign that maybe I should retire.'

'You're joking, right?' Alan stopped walking, incredulous. 'You'd give up the rock and roll lifestyle of a pub comedian because you lost your doll?'

'I told you, it's a sign.' Harry ignored Alan's jibe.

'I think people throwing their dinner at you might be more of a sign. Not losing your doll. Anyway, you'll probably find him at the hotel, sitting on the bar...'

'It's not a doll. He's a dummy.'

'Just like you'll be if you quit.'

'You're hardly one to talk.'

A barking dog interrupted Alan's reply. They looked across the road to where a German Shepherd dog was frantically pulling on its lead and yelping at a shop front, much to the embarrassment of its owner, who was apologising profusely to anyone who would listen.

'What's the matter with that dog?' Harry asked. 'He's going mental at his own reflection.'

Alan stifled a giggle. He could see Frankie pressed against the shop front as the dog growled at him. The owner desperately pulled on the lead in fear his dog would launch itself at the window. As the barking grew louder, he pulled the lead further back, causing the dog to stand on its hind legs as he fought back, the lead becoming increasingly taut.

Deciding that enough was enough, Frankie disappeared. The dog stopped barking, studied the now empty space in front of him and then ran off, dragging his relieved and confused owner behind him.

'What was all that about?' Harry asked, laughing.

Alan shrugged. 'Who knows? You know,' he added. 'I used to live next door to a German Shepherd. Every morning he would leap over my fence and take a dump on my lawn... His dog was just as bad.'

Harry shook his head. 'You shouldn't have given up your day job.'

Alan shrugged as they stopped at a crossing, waiting for the traffic to stop.

Frankie appeared next to Alan. 'Bloody dogs,' he moaned, following Alan and Harry across the road.

'So, what's the plan?' Alan asked.

'Ask at reception like a normal person,' Harry replied.

'Are you sure you can manage that?' Alan laughed. 'Go on then,' he added, gesturing Harry up the stone steps leading up to the large glass and chrome fronted building. 'After you.'

'Where have you been?' Alan hissed at Frankie. The ghost brushed imaginary dog hair from his velvet jacket.

'I'm not sure. I remember leaving your house, but instead of Sarah's office, I found myself outside that shop being menaced by a demented dog.'

Alan pulled a face. 'I don't think it's the dog's fault. All your popping in and out is enough to set anyone off...I'm tempted to bark at you myself.'

Choosing to ignore him, Frankie continued. 'So, what happened? What did I miss?'

'Sarah wasn't very helpful. She just told him to check with the taxi firm.'

Frankie frowned. 'You mean she didn't do all the work for you?'

'Exactly. It's about time she earned her ten per cent.'

'Ten percent of what you've earned recently is literally nothing,' Frankie pointed out. 'Anyway, heads up. Harry's back.'

Harry descended the steps. 'Everything OK?' he asked. 'I saw you talking to yourself.'

'Phone call,' Alan replied, pulling his phone out of his pocket. 'I was just following you up the steps when Sarah called. She wanted to know if you'd found him.'

Harry nodded. 'What did you tell her?'

Alan frowned. 'That we had only just got to the hotel... because we have.'

'OK. Let's go.'

Alan and Frankie exchanged looks and followed Harry back up the steps.

A ten-foot-tall Christmas tree laden with silver tinsel and white lights dominated the reception. Harry stopped in front of it.

'What's up?' Alan asked.

'I'm just checking Ernie isn't sat on the top like a fairy.'

'Mate. I know we were pissed last night, but I think it's extremely unlikely you climbed up there and planted Ernie on top.'

Harry stepped back, looking up. 'As I can't remember most of last night, I can't rule it out.'

Frankie sidled up to Alan. 'When I left you last night, you were struggling to stand up. There's no way either of you climbed up that tree. And if you had, you'd still be up there now crying because you don't like heights.'

'I can't see him,' Harry called out from the other side of the tree.

Frankie shook his head. 'For crying out loud.'

The receptionist looked up from her monitor and gave them a corporate smile. 'Good afternoon, gentlemen. How can I help you today?'

Harry placed his hands on the desk and leaned forward. 'We'd like to see the manager, please.'

Another smile. 'Do you have an appointment?'

Harry shook his head. 'I'm afraid we don't.'

The smile slipped fractionally. "He is extremely busy,' she warned. 'I'll see if he can see you...without an appointment.'

'Thank you,' Harry said. Alan flashed a smile.

'And you are?' She asked.

'Harry Hodges,' Harry said.

'Alan Rose,' Alan told her.

She tapped on the keyboard for a few seconds, then spoke. 'Hello, Mr Fulsack. There's a Mr Hodges and a Mr

Rose at reception to see you.' She paused for a moment, listening to the reply, then looked at them. 'Are you the comedians from last night?'

They both nodded.

'Yes, they are...OK, I'll let them know,' she ended the call. 'He says he'll be down to see you shortly. Please take a seat,' she gestured at a group of comfortable armchairs by a wall.

'That's promising,' Frankie said when they sat down. 'They haven't thrown you out yet. Hold on, here he comes.'

Alan looked across the reception. The manager, Ivor Fulsack, was talking to the receptionist. They took turns to glance towards Alan and Harry.

'He doesn't look very happy,' Frankie pointed out, somewhat unnecessarily, as Mr Fulsack glanced at them again, shaking his head.

Alan nudged Harry, who was reading a motoring magazine. 'Mate, that's him. The manager bloke.'

Harry looked up. 'Sorry Alan, what was that? I'm reading a fascinating article on the new Lexus SUV Hybrid.'

Alan rolled his eyes. 'You and I really have different ideas of fascinating.'

Harry shrugged and put the magazine back on the small table in front of him. 'What were you saying?'

Alan nodded in Fulsack's direction. 'That's the manager. I remember him from last night.'

'He's definitely not happy,' Frankie repeated.

'It can't be anything we've done,' Alan said. 'I was only

on stage for a few minutes. And no one listened to me anyway.'

'He's coming over now,' Harry said.

Mr Fulsack marched towards them. A sheaf of papers tucked under his arm.

'Hello,' Alan said, while Harry stood and offered his hand.

'Thank you for seeing us without an appointment,' Harry smiled.

Ignoring Harry's offer of a handshake, he said. 'If you'd like to come into the office, we can have a chat.'

'This is promising,' Frankie said. 'I bet he's got Ernie on his desk waiting for you.'

Ernie was not sitting on Fulsack's desk, nor was he sitting on a chair, or much to Harry's relief, stuck in the rubbish bin.

Harry looked around the office while sitting in the offered chair. 'He's not here,' he whispered.

Alan stole a look under the desk and shook his head.

Fulsack watched the two men looking round the office. One of them attempted a casual look under the desk. 'Are you OK?' he asked.

'Sorry, yes. I thought I'd dropped something.'

'Had you?'

'Had I what?'

'Dropped something?'

'No, I don't think so.'

'We'd like to speak to you about last night,' Harry said.

'I thought as much,' Fulsack replied. 'Go on.'

'Is there any chance I left Old Man Ernie here last night?'

'Who?' Fulsack asked, confused. 'Is that your dad?'

Alan snorted. 'Brilliant.'

'What? No. He's my ventriloquist dummy. Don't you remember, I had him with me last night?' Harry explained.

Fulsack sat back in his chair, stunned. 'I'm sorry. I thought you were here to apologise.'

Alan and Harry exchanged looks. 'Apologise? What for?' Alan asked.

'Never apologise, son,' Frankie said. 'Once a comedian apologises, he may as well give up.'

'These...' Fulsack tapped the sheaf of papers on his desk. 'Are just a few of the complaints I received this morning because of your efforts last night.'

'Ignore them,' Alan told him.

'Nice one, son,' Frankie said, approvingly. 'Well said.'

'We're comedians...' Alan gripped Harry's shoulder. 'We are the court jesters of our day, living on the edge of society. We seek truth in humour in a world beset with fake news and faux outrage. Every night we take to the stage like gladiators, knowing one misplaced word will see us cancelled. Whatever that means.'

Harry winced as Alan's grip tightened. 'Sorry mate,' Alan released Harry and stood up. 'You...' he addressed Fulsack. 'Have to stand up to these people. Tell them if they don't like cutting edge comedy, not to bother coming to gigs. Tell them if they want their comedy safe and unfunny to go to a Giles Monroe gig.' He sat down, pleased with himself.

'Well said, son,' Frankie said and gave him a round of applause.

Fulsack smiled. 'I tried to get Giles Monroe for last night. He's a very funny man. However, he is, unfortunately, very expensive. That's why we ended up with you two.'

Alan stared at Fulsack. 'What?'

'We couldn't afford him, so we had to take you two.'

Alan shook his head and slumped back into his chair. 'No wonder we couldn't connect with the audience. They were expecting vanilla, but they got salted caramel. We were second choice.'

'Third actually. Second choice was a fella who told jokes while juggling hedge trimmers, but he got injured a couple of weeks before. Apparently, a Christmas tree fell on him during a rehearsal.'

'Ned?' Harry asked and looked at Alan.

'We know him,' Alan pouted. 'Sarah never said we were third choice.'

'First, second, third or tenth choice, it makes no difference. You both alienated the audience and you...' He looked at Harry. 'Had several Christmas dinners thrown at you.' Fulsack paused for a moment to let the gravity of the situation sink in. 'I'm going to have to work extra hard to get their booking for next year. And now you two clowns turn up asking if you've left a ventriloquist dummy here.'

'Yes, Old Man Ernie. He's part of my act,' Harry told him.

Fulsack frowned. 'Ventriloquism is part of your act? I'm sure I saw your lips moving.'

'That's the point. It's meant to be funny.'

'I'm not sure it is.'

'Have you got him?' Alan asked impatiently.

Fulsack sighed. 'Have you got a picture?'

Harry fished his phone out of his pocket and scrolled through his photos. He handed the phone to Fulsack. 'Here's one of him with my fiancée, Katherine.'

The hotel manager studied the picture.

'Ernie's the one on the left,' Harry pointed out.

'I'm pretty sure I haven't seen him,' Fulsack handed the phone back to Harry. 'Where did you see him last?'

'We're pretty sure he was in the bar with us,' Alan said. 'But after that, it's a bit of a blur.'

Fulsack laughed. 'I understand you repaid your wages from last night back into the bar. I suppose I should be thankful for that.' He paused and then added. 'Why don't you look in at the bar on your way out? They might be able to help you.'

Harry offered Fulsack an insincere thank you, before leading Alan and Frankie out of the office.

Rather like the previous evening, Alan, Harry and Frankie were the first in the bar. They recognised the barman who was polishing glasses with a hotel branded tee-towel, inspecting them and placing them on a shelf.

'Hello,' Alan said. 'Remember us?'

The barman put down the tee-towel. 'Morning gents. If you two aren't carrying mega-hangovers, there's no justice in the world.'

'He definitely remembers you,' Frankie said.

'Did we leave anything here when we left last night?' Harry asked.

'Only your wages,' the barman quipped and laughed at his own joke.

'I, or rather we, were wondering if Harry here,' Alan gestured at Harry. 'Had left his ventriloquist dummy in the bar when he left last night.'

'Actually, it was earlier this morning,' Harry clarified.

'What's one of them when it's at home?'

'You remember...the small wooden child,' Alan said.

'Oh him,' the barman nodded. 'Yeah, I remember. You,' he nodded at Harry. 'Left with him. You had him under your arm.'

Harry turned to Alan. 'OK. Disappointing, but at least it's a starting point.'

'There's still a mystery to solve,' Alan said.

'Can I get you both a drink?' The barman asked.

Alan shook his head, and then added. 'Only if you can put it on Giles Monroe's account.'

FIVE

'...And you looked everywhere?' Sarah asked.

Harry nodded. 'We spoke to the manager, looked round his office and spoke to the barman who was on duty last night.'

'He can remember Harry leaving with Ernie,' Alan added.

'I looked on the top of the Christmas tree, just in case.'

'Just in case of what?' Sarah asked, looking at Alan for a hint. She received a shrug in response.

'Just in case he was on the top. Like a fairy,' Harry explained.

Sarah rolled her eyes. 'Oh right. Of course. How silly of me.'

'Why did you book Ned before us?' Alan asked, changing the subject, catching Sarah off guard.

'Because...err. Who told you?'

'The manager. He said he wanted to book Giles, but he was too expensive, so he booked Ned, but then Ned injured himself.'

'Right. Well,' Sarah began. 'I actually booked Harry with Ned. I just didn't book you.'

'Why?' Alan responded indignantly.

'Because you don't commit to anything. You refuse to accept anything that involves a journey, that needs a change of bus, and you won't play any venue that has a...' She made speech marks with her fingers. 'Bloody awful name.'

'That's rubbish,' Alan fired back at her.

'Is it? Last month, you refused to play at a comedy club called the Cross-Eyed Cabin Buoy. I didn't book you first because you're not reliable.'

'She's got your number,' Frankie laughed from the back of the office.

'But apart from that.'

Sarah laughed. 'Well, apart from that, you're fine.'

Alan slunk back into his seat, grumbling.

'So, Harry,' Sarah said, turning her attention away from the sulking Alan. 'Are you still available for your gig on Friday now you've lost your wingman?'

Harry chewed his bottom lip. 'I'm not sure I can do it without Ernie. Can I think about it and let you know?'

'Alan?' Sarah said.

'No.'

'You don't know what I'm going to say yet?'

'Well, before you even think about asking me, I can't cover for Harry on Friday. Get someone else to do it.'

'You know Ned's injured.'

'What about Beachy?'

'He doesn't like doing gigs during the Christmas period. He finds happy, laughing people depressing.'

'He should come to one of your gigs.' Frankie laughed.

Alan glared at Frankie.

'So,' Sarah continued. 'I'd really appreciate it if you could cover for Harry.'

'You see, the thing is, Friday is the Christmas party at the Cloven Hoof. It's a great night.' Alan explained, sitting back in his chair, satisfied his reasoning would end the conversation.

Sarah frowned. 'And you can't give it a miss to help your friends out?'

Alan shook his head. 'I missed year last because we were in Lapland. There's no way I'm missing it for a second year.'

Sarah knew the Cloven Hoof. It was Alan's local and ticked every box for a typical run-down pub. Tatty décor dating back to the eighties, threadbare carpets so sticky in places it was impossible to slip over, and suspiciously named drinks that made her doubt they had been purchased through any official channels. She turned her attention back to Harry.

'Come on Harry, I'm struggling here.'

Harry sighed. 'It just wouldn't be the same without him.' He finished his cup of tea, placing the empty mug on Sarah's desk. 'I'll go home and think about it. Hopefully, I'll find him before then.' He looked at Alan. 'I'll check the fridge again,' he added, before getting up to leave.

'Check the fridge again?' Sarah repeated once Harry had left the office.

'I told him to have a really good search round the house.'

'Listen Alan. If I have to let down another venue this close to Christmas, no one will take me seriously again. I'll struggle to get you booked in anywhere.'

'That's good, isn't it?' Alan said. 'A comedy agent who's not taken seriously. Better than one who's serious?'

'Let me explain something to you.' Sarah's patience was

wearing thin. 'If the agency goes under because the comedians are unreliable, no other agency is going to touch you with a bargepole. You'll be back in the Civil Service faster than you can say *performance targets*. And you'll probably end up at the bottom the pile again. Being ordered around by twenty-three-year-old graduates. Seriously, is that what you want?'

'She has a point,' Frankie said.

Alan raised his hands in surrender. 'OK, I'll speak to Harry, see if I can get him to commit without Ernie.'

'And if not, you'll cover for him?'

'I can't, it's...'

'Yes, I know, The Cloven Hoof's Christmas party.'

Alan stood up. 'I'll speak to Harry...' He paused. 'Do you want me to see if I can get you a ticket for the party? It's fifteen quid, which includes a buffet and your first drink free.'

Sarah glared at him. 'Alan?'

'Yes?'

'Get out.'

Rosie put her mug down on the coaster on the kitchen table. 'What do you mean he lost Old Man Ernie?'

'Exactly that,' Alan explained. 'He was a bit pissed when he left the hotel. We can prove Harry had him when he left the bar, but somewhere between there and home, he lost Ernie.'

'Why weren't you keeping an eye on him?'

'I was, but Harry left without me seeing him.'

Frankie guffawed from the other side of the room.

'Really?' Rosie arched an eyebrow.

Alan sighed. This was typical Rosie. Instead of accepting the situation, she was looking to blame him for not supervising Harry.

'Harry's a fully grown adult. He can look after himself.'

Rosie shook her head. 'But not a ventriloquist's dummy, it seems. It's not like a phone slipping out of your pocket. It's a knee height lump of wood.

'I know, but as I said, he was very drunk.'

'Is he OK?'

Alan sighed. 'He's not happy, No. He's talking about packing it in if he can't find Ernie. They're a double act. He can't perform on his own.'

Rosie nodded. 'Like Ant and Dec.'

'For crying out loud,' Alan groaned.

'Who are Ant and Dec?' Frankie asked.

'He's supposed to be doing a gig on Friday, but he won't commit to it and Sarah expects me to cover for him.'

'That's fair.'

Alan shook his head. 'No, you don't understand. I told Sarah, and Harry, I can't do Friday.'

'Why not?'

Alan sighed. 'It's the Cloven Hoof's Christmas party.'

Rosie frowned. 'You're always in that grotty place. Why is it any different to any other night? And Sarah's right. You should be helping Harry out.'

'Right,' Alan began. 'First, it's not a grotty place...'

'It *is* pretty grotty,' Frankie piped up.'

Ignoring him, Alan continued. 'Second, it's a special Christmas party. Invitation only. And third, I'm not in there that much.'

'Invitation only,' Rosie repeated. 'I doubt they'll sell out. No one in their right mind would spend any time in there. Plus, Harry's your friend. You should help him out.'

'Actually, I am helping Harry out,' Alan announced.

'How?'

'I'm meeting him tonight and we're going to work out a plan on either finding Ernie or doing a gig without him.'

Rosie eyed him suspiciously.

'Don't look at me like that. James is meeting us, too. I'm sure between the three of us we can come up with a solution that lets Harry do his gig, and I can get to the party.'

'So, it's a purely selfless act?'

'Exactly,' Alan said, nodding. 'Win, win.'

'Where are you meeting them?'

Alan grinned. 'The Hoof.'

SIX

James arrived at The Cloven Hoof to see Harry seated at their usual table on a raised area at the back of the public bar. James waved at Harry, then made his way to the bar and ordered two pints.

'You're coming to the Christmas party on Friday, aren't you, James?' Gary the landlord asked as he waited for a worryingly cloudy pint of beer to settle down.

'Definitely,' James patted his pocket. 'Got my ticket. I'm looking forward to it.'

Gary placed one of the pints in front of him. 'Are you taking part in the Secret Santa?'

James paid for the drinks. 'I didn't know you were doing one.'

'It's a last-minute thing. I thought it would be Christmassy.'

James considered this information for a couple of seconds before breaking into a broad grin. 'Why not? It's a great idea.'

Gary produced a battered ice bucket from beneath the bar. 'Here you go,' he urged. 'Pick a name.'

James stuck his hand in the bucket and pulled out a sandwich.

'Not that. That's my lunch. I've been looking for that.' He offered the bucket back to James and took a bite out of the sandwich.

This time James pulled out a scrap of paper, peering at the name scrawled in something that may well have been blood. Boris.

'Who have you got?'

James grinned. 'I can't tell you that. It's supposed to be a secret.'

'OK. But if you want to get them a bottle of vodka, I can let you have one at cost. Five pounds.'

'Fair enough.' James nodded and pulled a five-pound note from his pocket. 'Keep it behind the bar. I'll collect it on Friday.'

'Nice one, James.' Gary said. 'Good choice.'

James took the two pints and made his way over to Harry, threading between the empty tables and the one occupied by a sleeping Boris.

'So, you lost Ernie.' James said with a greeting, placing both pints on the table.

'I don't know what to do,' Harry admitted. 'I've looked everywhere.'

'Have you looked in the fridge?'

'Yes. Three times.'

James sighed and shrugged. 'I don't know what to say, mate. He must have done a runner.'

Harry sipped his pint and stared across the bar.

'I'll say this for Gary,' James said to change the subject. 'He's really tried to get this place ready for Christmas.'

Harry looked around the bar. An artificial Christmas tree stood on an upturned bucket in the corner. Silver tinsel wrapped around a sparse collection of branches appeared to be holding the tree together. Tatty paper chains hung at random places from the ceiling while behind the bar an advent calendar was pinned to the wall. Its little doors hanging open, the compartments already bereft of chocolate treats.

'Has he?' Harry questioned, taking another look around the bar in case he'd missed something.

James nodded. 'Definitely. He's pushed the boat out. To be honest...' James edged closer to Harry and lowered his voice. 'He didn't make much of an effort last year.'

'Didn't he?'

'It was very disappointing, just the Christmas tree and a bowl of roasted turkey's feet on the bar.'

Harry reached for his pint and wondered if he was having a nightmare.

The light snow that accompanied Alan and Frankie as they left home had turned into a swirling blizzard by the time they reached the Cloven Hoof.

Alan pushed the door open and stepped inside. A sign above the door asked him to wipe his feet before entering. Underneath someone had written in marker pen, *and on the way out*. While Alan stamped snow off his shoes, Frankie slipped past him and into the pub. Alan gave James and Harry a wave and made his way to the bar.

'You *are* coming to the party on Friday?' Gary asked as he poured Alan's pint.

'Wouldn't miss it for the world. I'm really looking forward to it.'

Gary placed Alan's pint on the bar, peered closely at

the contents. He frowned, stuck a finger in the pint, and gave it a stir. He removed his finger, licked it, and pulled a sour face as he poured the contents into the sink. 'I'll change the barrel and bring it over.'

Alan doubted a change of barrel would improve matters. 'Don't worry, I'll have a bottle.'

Gary opened the fridge and passed Alan a bottle of beer. 'Are you bringing your lovely girlfriend on Friday?'

He shook his head. 'No, she's not coming. She said she'd sooner have a smear test.'

'Very sensible,' Gary said. 'You can't take chances with your health.' He paused for a moment and leaned forward. 'Do you want to take part in the Secret Santa?'

'I didn't know you were doing one.'

'It's been a bit of a last-minute thing. I thought it would be Christmassy. Max spend a fiver.'

'Go on, then,' Alan said.

Gary produced the ice bucket from behind the bar and offered it to Alan, who put his hand in and pulled out a folded scrap of paper and a crisp.

'Who have you got?' Gary asked.

Alan smoothed out the piece of paper on the bar. 'James.'

Gary leaned closer. 'If you're stuck for anything to get him, I can let you have a bottle of vodka at cost. Five pounds.'

Alan chewed his lip. 'James doesn't like vodka.'

'Maybe not, but he can take it to parties or give it as a gift.'

'You're right. Excellent idea.' Alan dug into his pocket and pulled a five-pound note out of his pocket.

'I'll keep the bottle here. You can collect it from behind the bar on Friday.'

Alan nodded his thanks, grabbed his drink and made his way towards James and Harry.

'Did you find him?' Alan asked as he sat in a spare chair.

Harry shook his head. 'I'm afraid not.'

'He checked the fridge,' James confirmed.

'OK,' Alan took a swig from his bottle. 'In that case, we need a plan. Any ideas?'

Harry shrugged while James sunk into his chair and investigated the contents of his glass.

'So that's a no then, is it?'

'Well,' James began, drawing everyone's attention. 'We could...No it's a stupid idea...forget it.'

'What is it? It's not like we have anything else,' Alan said.

'What if I persuaded one of the year sevens to dress up as Old Man Ernie and stand in for him on Friday?'

Alan looked at him with contempt. 'You're right.'

'For crying out loud,' Frankie groaned and put his head in his hands.

'Am I?' James said, perking up.

'Yes. It *is* a stupid idea. Anyway, what self-respecting year seven would dress up and sit on *his* knee?' Alan nodded at Harry.

'I'm sure I can find a kid who would do it for an A in their next assessment.'

'Sorry James,' Harry said. 'I'm not passing a child off as Old Man Ernie. It's not right.'

James sighed and fell back into his chair. 'Well, that's all I've got.'

'Is this the best we can do?' Alan raised his voice.

'Keep the noise down please,' Gary called from the bar. 'There's people trying to sleep in here.'

Alan raised his hand up in a vague gesture of apology.

'Listen,' Alan whispered conspiratorially. 'We can think of something. Surely?'

Harry and James exchanged looks and shrugged.

'Well,' James began. 'I watched this documentary a couple of weeks ago about a family in America who moved house...'

'Is this going to be relevant?' Harry asked.

'Trust me,' James reassured him. 'Anyway, this family moved a thousand miles across the country and once they got to their new home, they realised they had left the cat behind.'

'And?' Alan asked.

'Well, they called their old house and spoke to the new owners and told them to look out for the cat. They heard nothing so they thought they'd lost it, but a month later they woke up in the middle of the night and their cat was sitting outside the front door, miaowing to come in.'

'Rubbish,' Frankie said.

'What's that got to do with Ernie?' Alan asked.

'Well, that cat had a homing instinct to find its owners. Maybe Ernie will turn up one day.'

'Like some kind of homing instinct?' Harry asked.

Alan frowned at his friend. 'A homing dummy?'

'Exactly.'

'Idiot!' Alan snapped.

'Any better ideas?' James said.

'That's not going to be difficult. We've set a very low bar,' Harry admitted.

Alan sighed and sat back in his seat. 'Well, that's just great. I'm going to miss another Christmas party here because I'm going to have to stand in for Harry at some grotty little dive just to save Sarah's bacon.'

'I'll get some drinks,' Harry announced, standing up. 'Same again?'

Alan and James nodded and mumbled their thanks. Alan adjusted his chair so Harry could squeeze by.

———

'Are you coming to our Christmas party on Friday?' Gary asked Harry as he pulled a pint.

'I'm not sure. I might be working.'

'That's a shame. It's going to be a great night.' He waited for the lumps of sediment to settle at the bottom of the glass and reached for another. 'Do you like Slade?'

'The band?'

'That's them. They're going to be playing their Christmas song live.'

'What? In here?' Harry asked.

'Well, it's their live Christmas album. James sold me the cassette.'

Harry nodded. 'Oh, right.'

Gary leaned forward. 'Why don't you take part in the Secret Santa? I'll put your name in the hat, and you can come along at the weekend and collect your gift.'

Deciding that agreeing would mean he could get away from the bar and back to his friends a little quicker, Harry agreed.

Gary pulled the bucket from under the bar and offered it to Harry, who reached in and took out a folded post-it note.

'Grace,' He read. 'Who's she?' Harry looked around the bar.

'That's her over there,' Gary nodded at the furthest corner. An old lady wearing two coats was asleep with her head resting on the table. She appeared to be using a packet of crisps as a pillow.

'I don't know her,' Harry pointed out.

'No reason you should. She hasn't spoken to anyone in seven years. Comes in every night for a glass of whisky and a nap.'

Harry nodded and paid for his drinks.

Gary leaned closer. 'If you're stuck for anything to get her, I can let you have a bottle of vodka at cost. Five pounds.'

'To be honest, I wouldn't know what to get her, so I'll take you up on that.' He passed a five-pound note across the bar.

'I'll keep the bottle behind the bar for Friday,' Gary told him and passed him a scrap of paper. 'Put your name on there and I'll put you in the Secret Santa draw.

Harry wrote his name on a grubby scrap of paper, handed it to Gary, placed the three pints on a tray and made his way back to his friends.

'You both look very pleased with yourselves.' Harry said as he placed the tray on the table.

'We had a great idea.' Alan told him.

'Really?' Harry said, unconvinced.

'There's a poster outside on the lamppost,' James said. 'You might have seen it?

Harry shook his head. 'No.'

'It's the one about the missing person.'

Harry took a gulp of beer. 'And?'

Alan grinned. 'When people find things, they take them to the police. Tomorrow morning, you and I will go to the police station and see if anyone has handed him in.'

'I suppose we've got nothing to lose,' Harry said.

'Trust me,' James said. 'It's a brilliant idea. What could go wrong?'

SEVEN

PC Andy Wen looked up from his screen to the monitor on the wall. 'Looks like we've got customers.'

The other officer manning the front desk, PC Ken Howe, looked toward the front doors. Two men stood in the waiting area that kept the public away from the front desk until they decided it was safe for them to be let in.

'What do you think?' Howe asked. 'Safe?'

Wen studied the image on the screen. 'Two men. One in his thirties, early forties maybe. The other older...' He looked closer. 'Maybe in his mid-sixties.'

'The older man is dressed like an off-duty accountant. The other...'

'Nondescript. No chance he's up to any funny business.'

'The question is,' Wen asked. 'Are they safe to be let in?'

Alan, Frankie and Harry stood in the airlock between the front doors of the police station and the front desk.

'Police stations have changed since my day,' Frankie said, looking around the waiting area. 'They used to be open twenty-four seven. Crooks don't work nine-to-five.'

'What do you think they're doing?' Harry asked, oblivious to Frankie's musings.

'Probably scanning us with all kinds of facial recognition software to see if we're trouble.'

Harry nodded. 'That makes complete sense,' Harry said, not understanding at all.

Alan grinned, warming to his theme. 'So, if you've got a criminal record, now might be a good time to do a runner. Once they've got you in there, there's no getting out.'

The door clicked and an intercom voice asked them to push the doors and step through.

'Good morning, officer,' Harry said cheerfully.

'Good morning, sir.' Wen said. 'What can we do for you today?'

'Well...' Harry began. 'I, or rather we,' he nodded at Alan. 'Are comedians, and we'd like to report a missing dummy.'

Ken Howe leaned against the counter. 'I'm sorry, a missing what?'

'Dummy.'

'A ventriloquist's dummy,' Alan clarified. 'Like a large doll.'

'And he's missing?' Howe sought clarification.

'Missing or lost?' Harry said. 'What's the difference?'

Wen sighed. 'Different forms.'

'How about mislaid?' Alan asked. 'Does that need a different form?'

Wen looked at Howe. 'Does it?'

Howe shrugged. 'Not sure. Let's go with missing and see where it takes us.'

'OK,' Wen tapped away on his keyboard. 'Let's take some details, shall we?' He waited for the form to appear on the screen. 'Right then. Name?'

'Ernie,' Harry said.

'Surname?'

Harry frowned. 'I'm not sure.' He looked at Alan.

'Hodges?' Alan mouthed.

Harry nodded. 'Hodges.'

Wen tapped the keys. 'OK Mr Hodges, when did you last see your dummy?'

'Ernie,' Harry said.

Wen nodded. 'OK Ernie, when did you last see your dummy?'

Harry and Alan exchanged confused looks. 'About two am Tuesday. We were at the Apollo Hotel in Hammersmith. We had a gig and went to the bar afterwards.' Harry paused while Wen tapped at the keyboard. 'I had him when I left but haven't seen him since.'

'How did you get home?' Howe asked.

'Cab. And yes, I checked. They don't have him.'

'So,' Wen began. 'At some point after you left the hotel, you mislaid...'

'Or he was taken...' Harry interrupted.

Wen gathered his thoughts. 'You haven't seen him since last night?'

Harry shook his head. 'No.'

'Have you checked the fridge?' Howe asked.

'Three times.'

Howe shrugged. 'I don't know what to suggest, then.'

'We were wondering if he had been handed in?' Alan asked.

Howe and Wen frowned at each other. 'I can check the lost and found log,' Howe suggested.

'That's great,' Harry said.

Howe sighed. 'Can you bear with me? There'll be

another form to fill in.' He tapped away at his keyboard. 'Can you give me a brief description of the missing item?'

'Well, he's about three feet tall. He's got brown hair, green eyes and was wearing a beige suit.'

Howe shook his head. 'Could be anyone...Any distinguishing features?'

'Yes,' Alan snapped. 'He's got a bloody great hole in his back.'

Howe tapped on the keys. 'Right, I'll just run a check and see what we've got.' He clicked the mouse and sat back in his seat, folding his arms. 'Won't be long,' he told them and sighed.

'It's just as well we're not reporting anything serious, like a mass murderer on the rampage,' Frankie said. 'By the time they'd found the right form, he would have wiped out the entire town.'

Alan stifled a laugh, receiving a glare from Wen in response. 'Something the matter, sir?' Wen asked.

'Sorry, officer. Just a touch of wind.'

Wen nodded and returned to his stationery order form.

'Here we go,' Howe announced as the lost and found form loaded on his screen.

'Have you got him?' Harry asked and leaned over the counter to get a look at the screen.

Howe pulled the screen slightly towards him. 'Now then. Let's have a look. What's been handed in over the last twenty-four hours...'

Wen joined Howe at the counter, looking over his shoulder at the screen.

'Two shopping trolleys,' Howe read from the screen. 'A six-foot Christmas tree. Artificial. One semi-automatic machine gun...'

'Not another one?' Wen interrupted. 'How many is that this week?'

'Three. The end-of-year charity auction of lost property will be interesting.'

'Are these guys for real?' Frankie asked.

'How tall did you say little Ernie was?' Howe asked while carefully studying the screen.

Alan leaned against the counter, trying to see the screen. 'About three feet.'

'Have you found him?' Harry asked hopefully.

Howe laughed. 'No, I was just trying to work how many little Ernie's standing on each other's shoulders would be as tall as the Christmas tree that was handed in.'

'For crying out loud,' Alan groaned. 'Do you have him or not?'

'It would appear not,' Howe said. 'Well, at least according to the lost and found form.'

'If you don't have him,' Harry moaned. 'Where is he?'

'There is one other possibility.' Wen looked from Harry to Alan.

'What's that?'

'He's been taken.'

'Sorry?' Alan queried.

'He's been kidnapped.'

'Kidnapped?' Harry repeated.

'Or dummy napped,' Howe added.

'Dummy napped? Is that even a thing?' Alan asked.

'Why not?' Wen said. 'What else is there? He's not a sheep, so he can't be rustled.'

Harry nodded. 'I suppose not.'

'How do we know if he's been kidna...Dummy napped?' Alan asked.

'Well sir,' Wen replied. 'You could receive a ransom demand.'

'Or maybe an ear,' Howe added helpfully.

'An ear?'

'Yes, part of an ear, or the whole ear, sometimes. I suppose it depends on how much they can saw off.'

'And along with the ear, you'll get a ransom demand,' Wen added.

'Once you get the ear and a ransom demand, pop back here and we'll get on it before you can say The Lindberg Baby.'

'Oh great,' Alan mumbled.

'OK.' Wen placed a notebook on the counter. 'Let's make a start.' He opened the notebook, taking a pen from a drawer under the counter. 'Can you think of anyone who'd take little Ernie? Any jealous rivals?'

Harry looked at Alan. 'What do you think?' He whispered.

Alan laughed. 'Mate. I don't think you've got any worries there.'

'No, officer.' Harry told Wen. 'I don't think there's any jealous rival who would want to take him.'

'No jealous rivals,' Wen repeated, writing this down in his notebook.

'Have you upset anyone recently?' Howe asked.

'You'd better get a bigger notebook,' Frankie grinned.

Harry frowned. 'Let me see. Probably the entire audience at the Apollo Hotel the other night. They threw their dinner at me.'

Wen turned the page and started writing.

'The barman at the Apollo Hotel seemed to have a problem with Ernie. Half the audience at the Pun-itentiary last weekend booed me off...'

'What about the other half?' Howe asked.

'They'd left before the interval,' Harry admitted.

Wen turned the page and continued writing.

'Then there was that incident at the *Funny Bone* for the Royal College of Orthopaedic Surgeons' Christmas party. They got very upset.'

Wen stopped writing and looked up. 'I think that, in the circumstances, we'll leave it there and perhaps wait for the dummy nappers to make their move.'

'I could give you several more suspects.'

'I'm sure you could. But in the circumstances...' Wen flicked through his notebook. 'I think we've got enough to be going on with.'

'So,' Howe said. 'If you gentlemen would like to be on your way...and don't forget to call us as soon as you receive an ear in the post.'

'Well, let's hope that doesn't happen,' Harry replied.

Wen looked down at his several pages of notes. 'Yes Sir,'

Ken Howe and Andy Wen watched as Alan, and Harry left the police station.

'What do you think?' Wen asked.

'I don't care what he says. A fiver says he'll find him in the fridge.'

Wen stroked his chin, deep in thought. 'I think you're right.'

EIGHT

'Look at that.' Alan thrust his phone under Frankie's nose. 'Six missed calls from Sarah. I wish she'd give me a break.'

'I think she might be stressed,' Frankie suggested.

Alan slipped his phone back into his pocket. 'I'll tell you what she's doing. She's trying to blackmail me into covering that gig. *"Oh, Alan, please help me out. We'll go out of business if you don't."'* Alan mimicked.

'Who was that supposed to be?' Frankie asked.

'Sarah. That was Sarah.'

Frankie nodded. 'Sorry, I didn't know she was Welsh.'

'What do you mean, Welsh?' Alan frowned at Frankie. 'Anyway, I have an idea about how to get Harry to cover that gig.'

'Which is?'

'I'm going to blackmail him.'

'How are you going to do that?'

Before Alan had time to explain, his phone rang.

'If this is Sarah, I'm going to ignore it.' Alan pulled his phone out of his pocket. 'It's OK, it's James.' He tapped the screen. 'Mate.'

'Hey, how's it going? Any joy at the police station?'

'No, but the officers we spoke to think he might have been dummy napped.'

'What?'

'Like kidnapped, but he's a dummy, not a kid.'

After a pause, James replied, 'Oh, OK. I think.'

'So, we're at Harry's now waiting for a ransom note with an ear attached to come through the letterbox.'

'Are the police there with you? Have they set up tracing equipment? You'll have to keep the kidnappers talking for thirty seconds while they trace the call.'

Alan looked around Harry's kitchen, which was totally devoid of police officers and tracing equipment.

'No,' he said.

Feeling disappointed that Harry's house wasn't the attention of the entire Metropolitan police force, James finished the call and hurried back to his class, who he said were failing miserably to learn Silent Night in readiness for the school Christmas concert.

Alan put his phone on the kitchen table. 'I think James is disappointed there aren't news crews camped outside and police helicopters hovering overhead.'

Frankie laughed. 'Hopefully an ear will turn up in the post and he'll get his wish.'

The kitchen door opened, and Harry walked in carrying a laptop, which he placed on the table. 'Katherine showed me how to put all my photographs on my laptop. Look.' He tapped a key to reveal a picture of Ernie wearing a cricket jumper. 'I thought if I printed some of these off, we could stick them to trees and lampposts. Like you do when a pet goes missing.'

Alan rolled his eyes. 'I'm sure that'll do the trick.'

Alan's phone rang again, interrupting further discussion. He scooped it off the table. Sarah again.

'Are you not getting that?' Harry asked.

'Er, yes,' Alan mumbled, and took the call. 'Hi Sarah. What's happening?'

'Alan, Hi. Where are you?'

'At Harrys. We've been out looking for Ernie.'

'Any joy?'

'None. The police think he might have been dummy napped.'

'What?'

'Du...'

'It doesn't matter,' Sarah interrupted. 'I need to talk to you. Can you come over to the office as soon as possible?'

Alan inwardly groaned. 'Do I have to? It's just that I'm giving Harry moral support in case an ear turns up.'

'This is important,' Sarah hissed down the phone.

Alan sighed. 'OK. We'll be over as soon as possible.'

'Just you. Not Harry.'

'What? Why?'

'I'll explain when you're here,' Sarah said, and hung up.

Alan pulled a face and pocketed the phone.

'What did Sarah want?' Harry asked.

'She wants me to go over and see her. I think she still wants to sort out Friday's gig.'

Harry closed the laptop. 'I'll get my coat.'

'No!' Alan said, a little abruptly. 'She said you should stay here and wait. Just in case a bit of Ernie turns up.'

'That's makes sense,' Harry said. 'So, Sarah is taking the dummy napping theory seriously?'

'Absolutely. She thinks it's the most likely explanation.'

Harry pulled out a chair and sat down. 'I'll wait for the

dummy nappers to make contact. Let me know what Sarah says.'

'Thanks for coming in,' Sarah said. 'I really appreciate it.'

Alan sat in one of the two chairs on the opposite side of the desk while Frankie sat in the other. 'You didn't really give me too much choice. What's the matter? And why so cloak and dagger? Why didn't you want Harry here?'

'What did you tell Harry?' Sarah asked.

'I said you thought it made sense for him to wait at home for a piece of Ernie to turn up.'

Sarah frowned. 'He doesn't think I buy into that ridiculous theory about kidnapping, does he?'

'It's not ridiculous,' Alan protested. 'It's the most likely scenario.'

'It's really not,' Sarah replied. 'He got drunk and lost Ernie.'

'I was with him. I would have noticed if we'd left Ernie behind.'

'By all accounts, you were worse than he was. The only surprise to this story is that you weren't found face down in a puddle, naked, having tried and failed to put Ernie's clothes on.'

Frankie laughed. Alan glared at him.

'Anyway,' Sarah continued. 'I didn't ask you to come here for an argument.' She laced her fingers together and leaned forward over the desk. 'I need to run something by you.'

'You're right, son,' Frankie said. 'She's going to blackmail you.'

Alan studied her carefully. 'Go on, then.'

'OK. When I was a little girl, I had a...'

'How old were you?' Alan interrupted.

'I can't recall...Five, maybe six. I don't remember. Is it important?'

'For context.'

Sarah sighed. 'OK, I was five and a half. Is that OK?'

Alan frowned. 'Yeah, that works. Carry on.'

'Thank you. When I was a little girl. About five and a half years old...' She paused and scowled at Alan. 'I had a pet hamster called Nigel...'

Alan sniggered.

'What now?'

'Nigel? Really?'

'I was five. Give me a break.'

'OK.' Alan grinned. 'Carry on with the adventures of Nigel the hamster.'

'I really loved him. He was my best friend when I was little. Every day waiting for me to get home from school so he could sit in his little ball and run round the living room.'

Alan nodded and stifled a yawn. 'And the point of this walk down memory lane is?'

'I'm getting there. Anyway, he lived to be ten years old, and when he finally died, my mum told me he was, in fact, the fourth Nigel. Apparently, Nigel had died several times over the years, and rather than have an upset child on their hands, my parents had simply gone to the pet shop and bought a Nigel replacement.'

'And you never noticed?'

'One black and white hamster looks very much like another when you're five.'

'Agreed. And the relevance of this is?'

'Oh, come on, son,' Frankie interjected. 'Keep up.'

Sarah chewed her bottom lip. 'We replace Ernie with an Ernie lookalike.'

Alan stared at her in disbelief. 'That's why you didn't want Harry here. You need my help in your subterfuge.'

'Listen, it's a small deception. Harry will have Ernie back, he'll do the gig, I'll be happy, you can go to the Christmas party at that slum, and you'll be happy too.'

Alan chewed his bottom lip. 'How do you plan on convincing Harry we've found Ernie when he's looked everywhere?'

'I'll tell him the hotel called me. They found Ernie, minus his clothes, stuffed in a bin earlier today after you'd both left.'

'Minus his clothes?'

'Well, unless we can find an identical suit to the one that Ernie was wearing, we'll have to return Ernie naked.'

'OK. Fair point. How do we explain away a naked Ernie? A very drunk dwarf needed a change of clothing?'

'We don't have to. Harry will be so glad to have him back he won't worry about the missing clothes. He'll accept whoever took Ernie took his clothes off as a prank.'

'A prank?'

'Yes, a prank. What do you think?'

'I think it's dishonest, and it's unfair to take advantage of a friend. Alan paused. 'On the other hand, it might just work, and if it does, you get to keep the agency going and I get to go to the Cloven Hoof's Christmas party. Let's do it.'

Sarah smiled. 'I thought you'd like it.'

'Where are you going to get an Ernie?' Frankie asked. 'I don't imagine they are that easy to get hold of.'

'Where are you going to get an Ernie?' Alan repeated.

'I've thought of that.' Sarah pushed the laptop round the

desk so Alan could see the screen. 'Look. I found two potential sellers, and neither is far from here.'

Alan looked at the image on the screen. 'The Puppet Palace,' he read. 'We stock all kinds of puppets and puppet accessories. Everything for your puppetry needs.'

'What do you think?' Sarah asked. 'Sounds like the type of place we'd get an Ernie lookalike.'

Alan nodded. 'You'd think so. What's the other place?'

'This one.' Sarah leaned across the desk and changed the image on the screen. 'Mr Giggles.'

Alan studied the screen. 'It's a joke shop. It says here they sell practical jokes and everything for the aspiring magician.'

'What do you think?'

'It's promising. What one do you want to try first?'

'Mr Giggles,' Sarah told him. 'It's closer.'

'OK.' Alan nodded. 'You'll pick me up in the morning?'

Sarah stood up. 'I've got a better idea. We'll go now. The sooner we find a new Ernie, the sooner we can all relax...Unless you have somewhere you'd sooner be?'

Alan sighed and followed Sarah out of the office.

NINE

'Get out! Go on, clear off. Get out of my shop.'

'Come on, Mr Giggles,' Alan protested. 'Don't be like that.' He ducked as a plastic dog poo flew over his head and went straight through Frankie.

'Steady on,' Frankie called out, slipping behind a display of magic wands.

'Mr Giggles.' Alan held out his hands. 'Can we just calm down a minute?'

'I told you. I'm not Mr bloody Giggles.'

'Why don't we all calm down for a moment?' Sarah said, stepping between the arguing couple.

'You.' He jabbed his finger at Alan. 'Get out,' he shouted. 'You're barred.'

Alan took a step forward. 'That's not fair. I've not done anything wrong.'

Another plastic dog poo flew past him and bounced off a mannequin in a full clown costume holding several balloons.

'Mr Gi..' Sarah stopped herself. 'Stop throwing things

and clam down,' she barked and turned to Alan. 'And you. Get out while I try to sort this mess out.'

'With pleasure,' Alan backed out of the shop and closed the door behind him.

'What was that about?' Frankie said. 'The guy went crazy.'

Alan shrugged. 'I have absolutely no idea. He went into full headcase mode, and I'd done nothing.'

'Do you think Sarah will be alright in there?'

Alan squinted into the shop. Sarah was in heated conversation with the shop owner.

'You'd better go in. Let me know if she needs any help.'

'So, you can dash in like a knight in armour and rescue her?' Frankie teased.

'No chance. The guy's a lunatic. I'll call the police.'

'Mr Giggles.' Sarah whispered. 'Why don't you tell me what the problem is?'

A vein pulsed on his forehead. 'I told you. I'm not Mr Giggles.'

'OK, OK. I'm sorry. But it says Mr Giggles on the sign outside and you are a Mister.'

The man sighed. 'That's just the name of the shop. I thought it was a fun name. For a fun shop.'

Sarah sensibly decided not to tell him he had failed. 'OK. What's your name?'

'Maurice Mooner,' he said. 'Most people call me Mo.'

'I'm Sarah,' she offered him her hand. 'I'm pleased to meet you, Mo.'

He shook her hand.

'So, why were you so upset with Alan?'

'Is that him?' Mo glared at Alan through the window.

'Yes, that's him. Did he do anything to upset you?'

Mo's cheeks flushed red again. 'Didn't you hear him?'

'Tell me again,' Sarah asked. 'I was too busy looking at your impressive collection of magic tricks.'

'He said that these...' Mo gestured at the rack of plastic dog poos. 'Were schoolboy practical jokes.'

'I see,' Sarah said, although she didn't.

'This is a serious joke shop. We provide all the great professionals with a full range of tricks.'

'Do you?'

'You know The Great Bongo?'

'No.'

'Well, we provide all his tricks.'

Sarah nodded. 'I see.'

'He,' Mo poked a finger at Alan. 'Insulted my professional integrity.'

'Well, I'm sure he didn't mean it. He's very aware of your reputation.'

'Really?'

'Yes. It was his idea to come here. To see if you could help us. He said, and I quote; *"Let's ask the people at Mr Giggles. They'll know what to do.""*

'I didn't know...sorry.'

Sarah smiled in triumph. 'It's fine. It was just a misunderstanding.'

'That's why I'm here,' Mo explained. 'I suffer from anger management issues.'

'Do you?' Sarah said. 'You wouldn't know it. You hide it so well.'

'A few years ago, my therapist suggested I make changes. Find less stressful work. Somewhere I could relax and be happy. I saw this place up for sale, so bought the lease.'

'And did it work?'

'Did what work?'

'Working here. Did it make you less angry?'

Mo pursed his lips and considered. 'I think so. Especially when there's no people. They're the ones who set me off.'

'When you say people, you mean customers. don't you?'

'Yeah. That's them.'

'OK,' Sarah sighed. 'My friend and I were wondering if you could help us with a problem.'

Mo looked out of the shop window to Alan, who smiled and waved in response. Mo twitched. 'What problem?'

'Well, the thing is, we were wondering if you had any ventriloquist dummies in stock?'

'Do you want one?'

'Well, yes, obviously. But it's not for us. It's for a friend. He lost his and we want to replace it.' Sarah pulled her phone out of her bag and swiped the screen several times. 'Look. This is what he looks like.'

Mo studied the picture on the phone. He sighed. 'I'll have a look in the stockroom, see if we've got any.'

'Thanks,' Sarah smiled politely while Mo hurried off to the back of the shop.

'Is it safe?' Alan called from the doorway.

'Shhh,' Sarah hissed, and hurried over to the front of the shop. 'He's gone to check if he's got one.'

'I wouldn't hold your breath, son, 'Frankie said.

'You really think he's going to help us?' Alan questioned. 'He threw plastic dog poos at me.'

'He's fine. You just rubbed him up the wrong way.'

The storeroom door opened. 'Stay here,' Sarah ordered, and shut the door before Alan could say anything further.

Mo put a box on the counter. 'I've got this one. It looks similar.' He took the lid off the box and gently pulled the dummy out. 'What do you think? Close enough?'

Sarah studied the dummy sitting on the counter. It had a shock of red hair, multiple scars tracked across his face, one ear looked to have had a lump bitten out of it and one of his hands had two fingers missing.

'I'm not sure. I've a niggling feeling that Harry, that's our friend, could tell the difference.'

'This is from the horror collection. It's very popular.'

Sarah gestured at the second box. 'Let's try that one.'

Mo opened the box and lifted the dummy out. 'What do you think?'

'One small difference I can see straight away.'

'What's that?' Mo asked.

'It's female. We need a male.'

Mo nodded. 'I suppose she is.'

Sarah shook her head. 'It's not really a question of *suppose*, is it?' She took another look at the macabre, disfigured doll. 'And you have nothing else?'

'I'm afraid not,' Mo leaned closer. 'To be honest, there's not much demand for them. They're not magic. And they're not jokes.'

'OK. We have another place to look at, so we'd better be going.'

'Where's that?'

'The Puppet Palace. Do you know it?'

Mo frowned. 'I know it, yes. I've always found them a bit, well, odd.'

'What do you mean, odd?'

'Peculiar. Weird. You know?'

Sarah looked at Mo. 'I think I know the type.'

‘What are they doing in there?’ Alan asked.

Frankie looked through the glass door. ‘They’re talking. Mr Giggles is showing Sarah a dummy.’

‘Really?’ Alan said, his interest piqued. ‘He could actually help. I take it back. This was a great idea.’

‘I’ll see what’s going on,’ Frankie said and walked through the glass door. ‘I told you not to hold your breath,’ he said a few seconds later.

‘What do you mean?’

‘Well, unless we can convince Harry that Old Man Ernie got run over by a combine harvester, I don’t think Mr Giggles is going to be of any use.’

‘Eh?’ Alan grunted, peering through the door. ‘I can’t see what’s going on.’

‘Don’t let him see you staring through the window,’ Frankie said. ‘Mr Giggles didn’t really take to you.’

Alan pushed his face against the glass. ‘I’m sure Sarah explained to that headcase that it was all a misunderstanding. When this is over, I’m sure we’ll be good friends.’

‘They say they have hundreds of dummies in stock,’ Mo explained.

‘Who says?’ Sarah asked.

‘Google. Look.’ He held his phone.

‘It’s OK. I believe you; I’ll check mys...’

‘He’s staring at me,’ Mo interrupted. ‘Look.’ He gestured at the front of the shop.

Sarah turned to see Alan's face squashed against the window. His nose deformed and flat, condensation expanding and receding as he breathed, his hand above his eyes to reduce the glare.

'I, err,' Sarah began. 'I think he's just trying to see what we're doing.'

Mo's face reddened, a vein on the side of his face throbbing. He grabbed a handful of plastic dog poos from the counter and marched towards the door. 'Wants to stare at me, does he?'

Sarah sighed and hurried after Mo. 'Remember what I said. He's a big fan of your shop.'

Ignoring Sarah's pleas, Mo pulled the door open and stepped out onto the pavement.

Frankie instinctively ducked behind Alan. 'He's not happy, son.'

Alan waved. 'Alright, Mr Giggles. How's it going?'

'I told you. I'm not Mr bloody Giggles.'

'Any plans for Christmas?' Alan said as a plastic dog poo hit him squarely on the forehead.

TEN

Alan pointed at his forehead. 'Look!' He jabbed a finger at it. 'There's a dent in my head.' He reached up, pulling the rear-view mirror toward him. 'I can definitely see a poo shaped dent.'

Sarah pulled the mirror back. 'Do you mind? I'm trying to drive.'

'I'm the victim of a violent assault. I deserve a little more sympathy.' He pulled the mirror back and studied his reflection. 'Yeah, definitely a dent. I've probably got a concussion.'

'Will you leave the mirror alone?' Sarah snapped, grabbing the mirror with a huff. 'You deserved it. You upset him.'

'That bloke must have thrown a dozen turds at me.'

'Probably,' Sarah said without interest while slowing at a junction.

'And you bought the lot.' Alan turned his head over his shoulder to get a better look at the cardboard box rocking gently on the back seat next to Frankie, who smiled back at him. 'Why?' Alan asked.

'I thought it best to keep him sweet. Especially after you upset him twice in twenty minutes. The last thing I wanted was him getting on the phone to the Puppet Palace and telling them not to speak to us.'

Alan mumbled something under his breath and sunk back into his seat. 'Are we there yet?'

'According to the sat-nav, it's just up here. 116 The High Street.'

'There it is,' Frankie called out. 'Over there on the right.'

'It's over there, on the right,' Alan repeated for Sarah's benefit.

Sarah slowed down and leaned forward. 'Are you sure? It looks like all the shops have shut down.'

Alan looked across the road. Sarah was right. Several of the shops were empty with To Let signs in the windows.

'There it is,' Sarah said and pulled into a space on her left. 'Look.' She nodded across the road. Between two empty and distressed shop fronts stood 116 The High Street. Or to give it it's proper name, The Puppet Palace.

Alan leaned across Sarah's lap to get a better look. 'Crikey. That's really grim.'

'Son, that makes The Cloven Hoof look like something from the Ideal Home Show.' Frankie said.

'Are you absolutely sure it's still open?' Alan asked. 'Only it looks really tatty.'

The double fronted shop window display held sun-bleached dusty puppets and cobwebs. A faded and peeling sign across the top of the shop announced the shop as The Puppet Palace.

'The website didn't say it had stopped trading. And anyway, Mo would have said.'

'Mo?'

'Mr Giggles.'

Alan shrugged. 'Oh, him.'

'They're probably undergoing a re-fit or something.' Sarah said. 'Look, there's a light on, so there must be somebody in there.' She opened the door. 'Come on. Let's see if they can help us.'

Alan shook his head, sighed, and climbed out of the car and hurried after Sarah, Frankie trailing behind him.

'It looks a lot worse close up,' Frankie said. 'In fact, I'd go as far as saying the empty shops on either side look in a better condition.'

'Grim, isn't it?' Alan repeated, sidling up to Sarah. 'Maybe we should leave some of those joke dog turds hanging around. Might improve the look of the place.'

'Don't be so negative. Look, they've got Christmas decorations up.' She gestured at a badly faded multi-coloured paper chain and a single string of fairy lights hung across the window.

'They've probably been there since 1959.'

'That was a good year,' Frankie said. 'I remember playing at the Morecambe Municipal Hall...'

'Not now,' Alan hissed.

'Pardon?' Sarah said over her shoulder.

'Nothing,' Alan replied, shaking his head at Frankie.

An assortment of down at heel puppets, clowns, knights, and an animal loosely resembling a donkey sat slumped in the window, their strings knotted around them. A hand drawn poster taped in three corners to the window read; SALE; BUY NOW PAY LATER. Underneath, someone had written *No Strings Attached.*

Leading the way, Sarah stepped up to the door, took hold of the handle and gave it a gentle push. It eased forward. 'There you go, still open.'

'Look at this place,' Frankie said, following Alan into the shop. 'It's like something out of The Twilight Zone.'

'It's more of a puppet's graveyard than a palace,' Alan gestured around the dusty shop. 'Look.'

Piles of battered cardboard boxes were stacked precariously in corners and on shelves. Small puppet hands poked out from under the lids as if they were trying to escape.

Alan lifted the lid from a box. Several puppets dressed as cowboys stared back at him, their strings twisted together. He reached in and pulled one out, its strings entwined with another puppet, bringing them out together. He dropped the tangled mess back in the box. 'This stuff hasn't been touched in years.'

'More chance of them having an Old Man Ernie,' Sarah said positively. 'All we have to do is find someone who works here.'

'Hello,' Alan called out and thumped the lid of the nearest stack of boxes. 'Hello?'

'Alan!' Sarah snapped. 'Don't be a hooligan. Haven't you upset enough people today?'

Stepping away from Alan, she called out. 'Excuse me... Is there anybody here?'

'What...Hang on.' A muffled voice came from the darkness.

Alan and Sarah exchanged looks. 'Who said that?' Alan asked.

'I'm coming,' the voice said, a little clearer.

'Where's that coming from?' Sarah asked.

'The booth.' Frankie said.

'In there.' Alan pointed at the puppet show booth in the corner.

'Hello?' Sarah called again, walking over to the booth.

'Be careful, it might be dangerous,' Alan said.

'Are you worried about upsetting the ghost of Mr Punch?' Sarah grinned.

'I would be if I were you,' Frankie said. 'Nasty little bugger.'

'Actually, yes.' Alan admitted and hurried after her.

Sarah stood on her tiptoes and peered into the booth. Alan leaned in next to her.

'I can't see any...'

A man shot up from the bottom of the booth. 'Hello,' he announced, startling Alan.

'For Fu....' Alan began before Sarah put an arm on his shoulder.

'Hello,' Sarah replied. 'We were wondering if you could help us.'

'What? Help you with what? Hang on a minute.'

'Is this guy for real?' Frankie whispered in Alan's ear. Somewhat unnecessarily, Alan thought as he took in the man in the booth.

The man looked as though he had just woken up, grey hair pointing in all directions, a ruddy complexion with a matching red nose and blood-shot eyes. He grinned manically. 'Sorry, you caught me unawares. I was just having a nap.' He looked past them at the empty shop. 'Before the afternoon rush.'

'We were wondering if you could help us,' Sarah said.

The man sighed. 'Do you need directions?'

'No, we'd like...'

He grinned. 'I know.'

'You do?' Sarah said.

'Oh yes, I know exactly what you want.'

'You do?' Alan repeated.

'You're not the first and you won't be the last. Smartly dressed couple.' He paused and gave Alan a second look.

'Well, at least *you* are,' he nodded at Sarah. 'You come in here, pretending to want something, but you're all the same.'

'We are?' Sarah said.

'All you want is the lease. Buy it off me on the cheap, and before me and the wife have got to the end of the road, you've knocked it down and put up a coffee shop.'

'Actually,' Sarah began. 'We are genuine customers.'

He stared at her.

'We'd like to buy a puppet,' Alan finished.

The muscles in the man's face slowly relaxed, his grin returning. 'Customers? You should have said...That's the way to do it,' he grinned, leaning on the ledge of the booth. 'What can I get you? As you can see, we have a wide range of stock.'

'Most of it untouched since 1974,' Frankie quipped, causing Alan to smirk.

A door in the far wall opened, and an elderly lady dressed in a long blue dress and apron hurried towards them. She had the same complexion and wild frizzy hair as the man. 'Did I hear someone say *customers?*' She shrieked.

'Yes, dear,' the man said. 'I was just dealing with them.'

'I don't think so,' she said, entering the booth through a flap in the back. 'Not in the state you're in.'

'This is my wife,' he said. 'Judy.'

Really?' Alan asked.

'Yes, really.' Judy turned to her husband. 'I've made you some sausages for your lunch. You leave these nice people to me.'

The man huffed and puffed and shuffled backwards out of the booth.

'I'm sorry about that,' Judy said. 'He's not been the same since business started going downhill.'

'Really?' Alan repeated.

'Kids aren't interested in puppetry anymore. They've got computer games that do everything they want. Our industry is dying.'

Sarah nodded. 'That's very true.'

'I mean, we used to be booked for months in advance for children's parties. Not anymore. We've had nothing for a year. The last show we did...'Judy sighed and shook her head. 'It went wrong.'

'Went wrong?' Alan asked. 'How?'

'It was awful. The kids rioted. They weren't interested in Mr Punch, so they threw things at him, called him a paedo and when he tried to close the booth, they set fire to it.'

Sarah nodded. 'I wondered where the scorch marks had come from.'

'In the end,' Judy leaned forward. 'He swallowed his swizzle.'

Alan winced. 'Nasty.'

'It was. It brings tears to my eyes just thinking about it. Now we just have the shop.'

Sarah looked around the empty space. 'Do you get much custom?'

'One or two customers a week.'

'Well, hopefully we can be the third,' Sarah added optimistically.

'Let's hope so,' Judy smiled sweetly. 'What can we do for you?'

Sarah explained how Harry had misplaced Old Man Ernie and that they were looking to replace him with an identical dummy. She showed Judy the picture of Harry and Ernie on her phone. 'Ernie is the smaller one,' she added helpfully.

Judy frowned, increased the screen photo size, and chewed her lip. She turned the phone round several times, put on glasses, squinted, and repeated the process. After what seemed to Alan an unreasonably long delay, Judy finally broke the silence. 'There's not a great demand for these dummies. And strictly speaking, they're not puppets.'

'So, you don't have any?' Alan asked.

'I never said that young man. Let me check the stock-room.' Judy replaced the glasses in her pocket and slipped backwards out of the booth.

'Do you ever get the feeling you're completely wasting your time?' Alan sat on a stack of boxes. 'If she's got one, it'll probably date back to the 1950s.'

'I think we could pass Harold Macmillan off as Old Man Ernie if we had to,' Frankie piped up. 'In the right light.'

Alan grinned.

'Something amusing you?' Sarah asked.

Alan shook his head. 'No, not really.' But continued to grin anyway.

The rear door creaked open as Judy stepped into the shop, holding a large, dusty box in her arms. She placed the box on a collection of haphazardly stacked larger boxes, which groaned under the weight, pushing yet more dust into the air.

'That looks promising,' Sarah said and glared at Alan.

'We've got a few upstairs, but there isn't much demand.' Judy wiped her sleeve across the lid, removing a layer of dust. 'I think this one might be the closest to what you're looking for, but I'm afraid it's been upstairs for some time.' She lifted the lid and pulled a dummy out. 'What do you think?' She asked, sitting the dummy on the edge of the box. 'It looks similar, doesn't it?'

'It definitely reminds me of someone,' Alan grinned.

'Not Old Man Ernie,' Sarah added.

Frankie looked over Alan's shoulder and laughed. 'I think we were better off with the horror doll.'

Alan shook his head. 'I've realised who he reminds me of. It's Winston Churchill.'

'Why on earth did you buy it?' Alan said as they drove home. 'What possible use are you going to have for a ventriloquist's dummy that looks like Winston Churchill?'

'I felt sorry for them. Their business is failing, and I thought it might give them a little hope.' Sarah exhaled, before adding, 'I know what it's like to have a business in trouble.'

'Blackmail time again,' Frankie grinned from the backseat.

Alan sighed and looked out of the window.

ELEVEN

'*...It's only six sleeps to the big day...Come on guys, admit it. You're not ready, are you?*'

A hand shot out from under the duvet, banged the top of the clock radio several times, trying to turn the volume down, before giving up and pushing the radio off the bedside table with a crash.

Alan braced himself for Rosie's angry arrival, realised that she must have left for work and went back to sleep.

Alan bowed to the royal box. A bouquet of flowers landed on the stage at his feet. 'Thank you,' he called out and waved. He took a step forward only to be showered in lingerie. 'Thank you...You're too kind.'

As the applause died down, the sound of a xylophone filled the auditorium. 'Can someone answer that phone?' Alan called out as the xylophone increased in volume.

'It's yours,' the audience shouted back as one, jerking

him awake. Alan sighed. This was typical. The best dream he'd had in ages, and someone had to spoil it.

Alan opened his eyes, pulling the duvet from his head. He sighed and swung his legs out of bed before padding down the stairs into the kitchen.

His phone was vibrating on the kitchen table. He picked it up and answered. 'Sarah.'

Alan. I've had a call from the hotel manager. He wants us to come back to the hotel. He says he has something to show us.'

Alan groaned. 'Slow down. It's far too early for this many words. Can you call back this afternoon?'

'It's eleven thirty!' Sarah snapped.

Alan looked at the clock on the wall. It said eleven twenty-five. 'Eleven thirty-ish,' he replied.

'Anyway, I've been at my desk since eight thirty-ish and I'm due a break. I'll pick you up in half an hour.'

Alan sighed and headed for the bathroom.

'It must be good news, mustn't it?' Harry said for the third time since Sarah had picked him up. 'I mean, he wouldn't ask us to come over if he had nothing to say. *"Thank you for coming, I've got nothing to tell you. Bye,"* he mimicked.

Sarah nodded agreement. 'You'd think so, wouldn't you...Alan?'

Alan tore his gaze from the window. The Christmas themed shop windows had alerted him to a more personal issue. 'Yes, absolutely. No point in us going all this way if they haven't found him.'

Sarah glanced over her shoulder. 'What's the matter?'

'Err...What?'

'You agreed without trying to be funny or sarcastic. Are you ill?'

Alan slumped down in his seat. 'I don't know what to get Rosie for Christmas.'

Harry leaned forward between the front seats. 'What did you get her last year?'

'I got her one of those experience packages. '

'That was a lovely idea, Alan,' Sarah said. 'What was it? Spa weekend. Massage? City break?'

'A morning's falconry.'

'A what?'

'It was one of those sanctuaries for birds of prey. You turn up, pop on a leather glove, hold your arm out and this dirty great bird sits on your arm.' He thought for a moment, to recall the details. 'The bird keeper swings a piece of meat around and the bird...I think it was a falcon...or a kestrel... flies off your arm, grabs the meat and brings it back to you.'

'I didn't know Rosie liked birds of prey,' Harry said.

'She doesn't.'

Sarah frowned. 'Then, why?'

Alan shrugged. 'I thought she might like it. Maybe take it up as a hobby.'

'Did it work?' Harry asked. 'Only, she's never mentioned it.'

'She hasn't been yet. In fact, she hasn't mentioned it... ever.'

Sarah shook her head. 'I suppose it's the thought that counts.'

'Exactly.'

'And how are you going to top that?' Harry asked mischievously. 'I mean, you've set the bar high.'

Alan sighed. 'That's the problem. I'm short of inspiration this year.'

'Don't worry,' Sarah reassured him. 'I'm sure you'll be able to hit those depths again. You've still got a few days.'

'I hope so. I wouldn't want to disappoint her.'

Alan, Sarah, and Harry squeezed into the hotel manager's office.

'I'm sorry to drag you in,' Ivor Fulsack apologised. 'It's just there's something I thought you should see.'

'Have you found him?' Harry asked eagerly.

Fulsack leaned back in his chair. Sarah sat opposite in one of two chairs. Harry sat on the other while Alan fidgeted on the chair's arm.

'No, I'm afraid not. I asked you to come in because I wanted to show you this.' Fulsack tapped at his keyboard and turned the screen round.

Sarah leaned forward. 'What am I looking at?'

'This...' He tapped the screen with his pen. 'Is CCTV footage from outside the hotel from the other night.'

'The night Ernie went missing?' Harry asked.

'The night you lost him,' Alan corrected, receiving a kick under the desk from Sarah.

Sarah, Alan and Harry studied the image on the screen.

Harry frowned. 'I can't see anything. It's just a grey haze.'

Fulsack pulled the screen around and tapped on the keyboard. 'This should do it.' He offered the screen back.

The image, whilst still grainy, was a little clearer.

'Is that me?' Harry asked.

The image showed the front of the hotel. A clock in the top right-hand corner confirmed the time and date.

'Look,' Alan said. 'You've got Ernie.'

On the screen, Harry emerged from the hotel, stopped at the top of the steps and swayed. Reaching out, he took hold of the wall for support.

'Harry,' Sarah groaned. 'You look awful.'

Harry chewed his bottom lip.

'At this point you still have the dummy,' Fulsack pointed out.

The CCTV footage continued. Harry, with Ernie under his arm, made his way uneasily down the steps. Once he reached the bottom, he put Ernie on the bottom step and walked to the kerb.

'What am I doing?'

'If you're about to jump, it's a rubbish suicide attempt,' Alan quipped.

'Alan!' Sarah snapped. 'Don't be so insensitive.'

'Well...' Alan mumbled. 'It is. That kerb is only a couple of inches high. Look...'

On screen, Harry stood on tiptoes on the edge of the kerb. 'I'm looking for something.'

'Or waiting for something,' Fulsack suggested. 'Look.'

A car emerged from the left of the screen, crawling to a stop alongside where Harry stood. The driver's window opened. Harry leaned in, stepped back, opened the rear door and got in. The car then pulled away, disappearing to the right of the screen.

'I left Ernie behind,' Harry groaned.

'That must have been the mini cab,' Sarah added.

Alan turned to Fulsack. 'I don't suppose you checked outside to see if he's still there?'

Fulsack tapped on the keyboard again. 'Look. This is at five thirty that morning.'

On the screen, a bin lorry pulled up outside the hotel, its flashing light illuminating the entrance. A figure wearing a high–vis jacket jumped out of the passenger side and pulled a wheelie bin to the kerb. He repeated the process for two more bins before reaching the hotel's entrance.

'I've got a bad feeling about this.' Harry leaned closer to the screen.

The binman paused, staring at Ernie sitting on the step.

Harry winced. 'No...'

'This really is writing itself,' Alan said.

The binman reached down, picked Ernie up from the step, showed him to another binman, laughed and casually threw the dummy into an open wheely bin.

'No!' Harry exclaimed. 'He can't do that.'

'You're right, mate.' Alan said supportively. 'I think that's the paper and card recycling bin.'

Sarah glared at him. 'If you can't say anything constructive, please don't say anything at all.'

Alan put his hands up in surrender. 'Sorry, just trying to lighten the mood.'

Fulsack stared at the squabbling trio and sighed. 'Look, it's a bit of a long shot, but our rubbish is taken to the recycling centre in Wandsworth.'

'You think they'll let us look for Ernie?' Harry asked hopefully.

'Hey,' Alan punched Harry's arm. 'That's enough of the us. You're on your own with that.'

Fulsack shrugged. 'I'm not sure Councils let you rummage about in their rubbish tips, but you won't find out unless you ask.'

Sarah nodded. 'Very true.' She stood up. 'Mr Fulsack. Thank you for sharing this with us. We're very grateful.'

Fulsack stood. 'If you need me to speak to the people at the tip, ask them to call me. I'll tell them you were guests and some of your valuables were accidentally thrown away.'

Nodding her thanks, Sarah gestured at Alan and Harry. 'Come on boys, time to get your hands dirty.'

Harry got to his feet. 'Come on, Alan,' He urged, tapping his friend on the shoulder. 'Let's see if we can find Ernie.'

'Must we? 'Alan grimaced. 'It's going to be horrible.'

'Yes, we must,' Sarah said. 'Anyway, it might not be that bad. You know what they say about rubbish?'

'It's dirty and likely to give you a disease?'

'No. One man's rubbish is another man's treasure.'

Alan exaggerated a sigh and stood. 'Another man's treasure, you say?'

Sarah nodded. 'Yes.'

'Best get a move on, then. I might be able to find a Christmas present for Rosie.'

TWELVE

'The Shining Beacon Community Recycling and Waste Collection Centre,' Alan read from the signpost. 'Next left.'

Sarah reduced her speed before turning left into an industrial estate.

'They can call it whatever fancy corporate name they want, but a dump is a dump.'

'Or a tip,' Harry added.

Alan nodded. 'Yeah, a tip.'

'Finished?' Sarah asked.

'Not yet. It doesn't matter what grandiose title they give it. It's still going to be a massive steaming pile of crap. Rotting meat, mouldy vegetables, dead foxes, and the occasional body part.'

'What?' Sarah glanced over at him.

Alan sighed. 'Body parts. Like a hand or an arm. Or a foot. You see it all the time on crime shows. Some Stig will be shovelling the rubbish into a big pile, and he'll find a foot…'

'A Stig?' Harry asked.

'Stig of the Dump,' Alan explained.

'Give me strength,' Sarah mumbled.

'Actually,' Alan continued. 'If I find a foot, do you think they'd let me keep it?' I could give it to Rosie as a Christmas present.'

'Why?' Harry asked. 'Why would you give her a foot?'

'Well, you know how people use shoe inserts to keep the shape of their shoes when they're not being worn? Well, I reckon it would be cool if Rosie had an actual foot to put in her spare shoes.'

Sarah shook her head. 'I'm not sure "cool" is the right word. Perhaps macabre, gross or in poor taste are more relevant.'

'It would be a great conversation piece,' Alan said. 'Can you imagine the look on her face on Christmas morning?'

'I imagine she'll be speechless,' Sarah said, reversing into a parking bay.

'You can't just wrap up a foot and leave it under the tree. You'll have to preserve it,' Harry said.

Alan chewed his lip. 'Maybe I could bake it, like a clay pot, and then seal it with lacquer or something.'

'What size shoes does Rosie take?' Sarah asked.

'Eh?'

'There's no point giving her a size twelve foot if she takes a size four shoe. It wouldn't fit.' She paused and groaned. 'Look what you've done to me...' Head in hands, she groaned again. 'I've turned into you...I'm meant to be the sensible one, but you've turned me into an idiot.'

Alan gently placed his hand on her shoulder. 'Will you be wanting a ticket for the Cloven Hoof's Christmas Party?'

Alan spoke into his phone as he leaned against Sarah's car. 'No mate, listen to me. Ernie hasn't been stolen...'

'You mean dummy napped.' James interrupted from the other end of the line.

'Dummy napped. Rustled. Stolen. It doesn't matter. It's nothing like that.'

'Where is he then?'

Alan rolled his eyes. 'That's what I'm trying to tell you.'

'Go on then.'

Sighing, Alan said. 'It turns out Harry left him outside the hotel when he got in his cab the other night, and in the morning the bin men turned up and threw him in the rubbish.'

'Bloody hell. How did you find that out? Did Harry remember?'

'The hotel manager saw it on the CCTV and called us in.'

'So, can Harry do anything about it? I mean, it's not like he's going to rummage round the tip, is it? He's not that desperate.'

'Funny you should say that.' Alan glanced at a block of portacabins on the other side of the car park and sighed. 'We're at the rubbish dump now. Sarah and Harry are trying to persuade the manager to let us look through their rubbish.'

'Really? You realise it's going to stink, right?'

'Yeah, I'd kind of figured that.'

Across the car park, the door to the portacabin opened. Sarah stepped out, followed by Harry and a very short fat man wearing a high-vis jacket much too big for him and an oversized hard hat which rested on his ears.

'I'd better go. I'll let you know what happens.' Alan

pocketed his phone, smiling as Sarah approached. 'Everything OK?'

'This is Mr Skip. He's the manager. Sarah gestured at the man in the high-vis jacket. 'I've explained our position, and while he can't let us sort through the rubbish ourselves...'

'Health and safety,' Skip interrupted.

'Yes, for health and safety reasons. He is prepared to let us watch while his team of highly trained operatives scour the resource for us.'

'Resource?'

'Rubbish,' Harry confirmed.

Alan nodded. 'I see. And you've explained our position?'

Sarah glared at him. 'Yes. I explained about Harry losing his priceless family heirloom.'

'Priceless,' Harry agreed.

Skip spoke. 'We have strict health and safety rules at this site. Look...' He pointed at a sign by the kerb which proclaimed it had been "Twenty-three days since a fatal accident."

'We're hoping to get to twenty-eight days. It'll be a new record,' Skip said.

'I'd be happy with twenty-four,' Alan quipped while Harry smirked.

'If you'd like to follow me,' Skip headed out of the car park.

'Does he know that the family heirloom is, in fact, a ventriloquist's dummy?' Alan whispered.

'Shush,' Sarah hissed.

'He doesn't know, does he? I bet he thinks it's jewellery or a candlestick. Something with sentimental value.'

'Ernie does have sentimental value to me,' Harry hissed back.

'I'll let you explain that to Mr high-vis,' Alan whispered.

Sarah turned round and pressed her finger against her lips. 'Shush.'

Skip led them along a one-way road which opened onto a large area the size of a football pitch. Ten shipping containers lined up symmetrically in the middle, with a further ten containers lined up behind them. The road circled the containers before feeding back into the main complex.

'Our wagons come in here.' Skip pointed back the way they had come. 'They reverse up to one of the dumpsters, unload the rubbish and head back out. Normal household and commercial waste are dumped here while recycling, papers, card, plastic, metal. All the usual is in the containers opposite. Unfortunately, we don't have a special container for accidentally lost family heirlooms...'

Two men, one freakishly tall, the other barely five feet, but almost as wide, in high-vis jackets, each brandishing a long-handled rake, strolled toward them looking like health and safety gladiators. Skip nodded a welcome to his colleagues and continued. 'My operatives here will start a search of the containers. Please follow them and let them know what you're looking for.'

'We'll start at that end,' the tall man nodded to his left and wandered off, expecting everyone to follow him.

Alan watched Sarah and Harry trail behind them. 'You can come with me,' Skip said.

'What?'

Skip sighed. 'The girl, Sarah, is it? Said your heirloom was accidentally thrown in a hotel's rubbish chute. If it came in early on Tuesday, there's a chance we've already been cleared it and sent to the landfill pile. We can have a quick look there.'

'Oh,' Alan mumbled. 'Where's that?'

'Over there,' Skip pointed over Alan's shoulder.

Alan turned. Beyond the containers and the neat, ordered part of the centre, bordering on the riverbank, stood a large mountain of rubbish.

'What's that?' Alan asked, despite fearing he already knew.

'More rubbish. Waiting to be collected and taken down to Tilbury for land fill, incinerating and whatever.'

'Must we?'

Without replying, Skip set off back across the car park.

'Great,' Alan huffed and set off after him.

Alan watched a seagull swoop down onto the mountain of rubbish, peck at something and fly away. From his vantage point–leaning against a floodlight pylon - he couldn't see exactly what had attracted the seagull's attention, but within seconds, two more seagulls had arrived on the scene, pecking and squawking at the stinking pile of rubbish.

Skip used his shovel to turn over the edge of the rubbish pile, occasionally pushing something toward Alan, who shook his head. Skip sighed and returned to his task.

An icy breeze forced an involuntary shudder from Alan, as Frankie appeared next to him.

'Son, I've seen you play some dumps in your time.' He nodded at the rubbish pile. 'But this takes the biscuit.'

'Where have you been?'

'Overslept...I think. You know what it's like.' Frankie gestured at the mountain. 'Why?'

Alan sighed. 'Ernie hasn't been kid...dummy napped. He ended up in the rubbish when Harry got drunk. That's why we're here, looking for him.'

'I assume that's the condensed version?'

Alan nodded. 'You turn up late, you only get the potted history.'

'Oi, mate,' Skip called out and held up a candlestick. 'This it?'

'No,' Alan called back. 'I told you; it's shaped like a small child.'

Skip threw the candlestick back onto the mound of rubbish and carried on digging.

Frankie frowned. 'A candle stick shaped like a small child. What?'

'I'll explain later.'

Frankie looked at the sky. 'I leave you alone for a morning and look at the state of you, digging around a rubbish tip.'

'Hang on, he's coming back. Maybe he's found something.'

Skip shuffled his way through foothills of rubbish toward them, shovel in one hand, something odd looking in the other.

'What's that in his hand?' Alan asked.

Frankie squinted. 'Not sure. It doesn't look like Ernie, though.'

'I found this,' Skip said, holding out a candle stick covered in matted clumps of hair, suspicious stains and wrapped in a banana skin. 'Are you absolutely sure it's not the one you're looking for?'

Alan thrust his hands into his pockets, stepping back, desperate to avoid any contact. 'To be honest, no. It's not even remotely child shaped.'

Skip removed the banana skin and rubbed the candlestick on his jacket. 'Think I'll keep this for the office. It'll scrub up nicely.'

Alan rolled his eyes. 'Yes, very nice. Any chance we could get back to the task at hand?' He pointed at the rubbish tip.

'I think we'll call it a day. We would have found your heirloom if it had been dumped here a couple of days ago.'

'Did you see anything else that might be of interest?' Alan asked.

'What do you mean?'

'I don't know...' Alan paused and pinched his chin between his thumb and finger as if deep in thought. 'Something like a ventriloquist's dummy?'

Skip shook his head. 'Nah, nothing like that. Why?'

'No reason.'

Skip thrust the candlestick at Alan again. 'Sure, you don't want this?'

Alan shook his head. 'No, you keep it. It's not what we're looking for.'

'Great, ta,' Skip said and rubbed the candlestick on his jacket.

'Anything?' Harry asked as Alan approached.

'Nothing. Although perhaps we may have been more successful if he was looking for the right thing. He kept stopping to show me candle sticks.'

'At least they looked,' Sarah said. 'We wouldn't even have got this far if they'd known what we were really looking for.'

'So, we're back to square one,' Harry said.

'I can't believe you lot,' Frankie said. 'Where's the never say die attitude? The Dunkirk spirit? If Tolkien had this attitude, the Lord of the Rings would have been a short story. You're on a quest. Giving up is not an option.'

Alan gave him a cursory glance. 'Let's give up then. It's cold and I want to go home.'

Sarah put her hand on Harry's shoulder. 'Don't worry, we'll think of something.'

———

Twenty minutes later, Skip watched as a refuse lorry reversed up to a container and emptied its load. He ticked a couple of boxes on his clipboard before approaching the driver's cab.

'Do the usual,' he said, passing the clipboard through the open window.

The door opened, and the driver stepped down. 'There you go,' the driver said, passing the clipboard back.

'Ta.' Skip tucked the clipboard under his arm. 'What's this?' He asked, pointing at the front of the lorry.

'Our new mascot,' the driver told him. 'We found it and retired Garfield.'

Skip studied the new mascot tied to the lorry's radiator grill. 'What is it? It looks a puppet.'

'Jacko found it the other night. He thinks it's a ventrilo-quist's dummy.'

'Is it valuable?'

'Doubt it.'

Skip shrugged. 'No, I suppose not,' he said and saun-tered back to the office.

THIRTEEN

Alan opened the front door and stepped into the hall.

'Kitchen,' Rosie called out.

'Was that an order or a helpful clue where she is?' Frankie asked.

'Probably an order,' Alan whispered. 'Unless she's about to win at Cluedo.'

He led a chuckling Frankie along the hall and into the kitchen. 'Hi honey, I'm home.'

Rosie looked up from the pile of Christmas cards on the kitchen table and wrinkled her nose.

'Is that you?'

Alan dumped his phone and keys on the table. 'Is what me?'

'That smell,' Rosie's nose twitched. 'It smells like rotting fruit.'

Alan lifted his hoodie to his nose. 'Might be me. I was at a rubbish dump this afternoon.'

Rosie slipped a card into an envelope and sealed the flap down. 'I suppose I should ask why you were at a rubbish dump?'

Alan flicked the switch down on the kettle. 'Tea?'

'Coffee.'

Alan grunted and reached for two mugs. 'Go on, ask why.'

Rosie sighed. 'Why?'

'We were looking for Old Man Ernie.'

'Why?'

For the second time that afternoon, Alan explained the mornings events.

'Did you find him?' Rosie asked.

Alan poured boiling water over the coffee granules in the mugs, splashing the counter sloppily. He added milk with the same care and passed a mug to Rosie. She placed it on a coaster and sighed. 'Such care and effort.'

'No, no sign of him.'

'So, what are you...or rather Harry, going to do?'

Alan shrugged and dropped into a chair opposite her. 'What are you doing?'

'You mean apart from writing these Christmas cards?'

Alan gazed at the neat piles of cards and envelopes on the table and smiled. 'I wondered what they were.'

Rosie slid an envelope across the table. 'Here, you can deliver this one. Ideally before April.'

'It's addressed to Amy and James.'

'Yes.' Rosie replied patiently. 'Can you remember last year? I asked you to give them a card, which I should add, I bought and wrote. You had one job. Give the card to James during one of the many drunken nights you spent together in the week leading up to Christmas.'

'And?' Alan asked innocently, although he suspected where this was going.

'And can you remember exactly when you gave it to him?'

Alan screwed his face up in mock concentration. 'Was it just after Christmas?'

'Easter! You gave him the card at Easter. And that was only because I found it under the passenger seat of my car on Good Friday.'

'I told you what happened. I put it under there for safe-keeping when we were at the shops and forgot about it...' He paused.

'What?'

'Easter was late this year, wasn't it?'

'I think so. Why?'

'Then I wouldn't bother giving them this one. Last years is probably still up.'

Rosie opened another card and began writing. 'You could deliver it now if you like,' she suggested without looking up.

Alan picked the card up and turned it over. 'I'll give it to James when I see him next.'

Rosie looked up from the card she was writing to a relative that Alan had never met and stared at him.

'Trust me, it'll be stuck to their fridge with a magnet before you can say Happy Easter,' he teased.

'Are you sure you won't forget? One late Christmas card is embarrassing. Two late Christmas cards are unforgivable.'

Alan waved the card in the air. 'Trust me, I'm seeing him on Friday at the Hoof's Christmas Party. I'll give it to him then.'

'No!' Rosie snapped. 'Absolutely not. Once you step inside that place, you lose what little common-sense you have. You'll be a mess. There's no way James will take it home. You'll end up using it as a crisp plate.'

'Harsh,' Alan said indignantly.

'But fair,' Frankie added.

'Are you sure you won't deliver it now?' Rosie asked as she added another card to the pile.

'I'm sure. You're just going to have to trust me on this.'

Rosie nodded. 'OK, fine. It's probably for the best.'

Alan frowned. 'Why the change of mood?'

'Well...' Rosie put her pen down and leaned forward. 'When I went shopping with Jayne the other day, she bought a pair of shoes. She said she would bring them over tonight with some dresses and we could see which one goes with them.'

'Thrilling. I'll stay out of your way.'

Rosie shook her head. 'No, I expect she'll want your views too. It's good to get a man's perspective on these things.'

Alan picked up the card. 'I'll tell you what. I'll deliver the card now.'

'You said you'd give it to James when you see him next.'

Alan stood up. 'No. The more I think about it, the more concerned I get that I could forget. You never know what could happen between now and Friday...I'm also anxious about Old Man Ernie. If I'm not concentrating, I could forget about the card.'

'Well, if, you're sure?' Rosie said innocently. 'Jayne will be sorry she missed you.'

'Can't be helped. Duty calls.' Alan slipped the card into the pocket of his hoodie and headed towards the front door. 'I'll be as quick as I can, but don't wait up.'

Rosie picked up the pen and went back to the Christmas cards. The front door shut, and she smiled. 'Sucker.'

'He's upstairs,' Amy said by way of a greeting, holding the front door open.

Alan and Frankie filed past her and into the hall.

'Happy Christmas,' Alan said, offering her the envelope. 'Here's your Christmas card.'

'Are you sure?' She asked. 'It's not Easter for a few months yet.'

'That's why I'm here. I thought I'd deliver your card personally, rather than leave it for Rosie.' He rolled his eyes. 'To be honest, she's a bit unreliable on the whole Christmas thing.'

Amy gestured up the stairs with the card. 'He's in his den.'

Alan began climbing the stairs. 'Thanks,' he called back from over his shoulder.

For a fraction of a second, Amy thought she saw another figure following Alan up the stairs. In the time it took to open her mouth the thought left her. She shook her head and put it down to overwork and the presence of her husband's stress inducing best friend.

Alan led Frankie along the landing and through the open door.

'Alright,' James mumbled without looking away from his games console.

'Does Amy know that you're looking at this filth?' Alan said in a voice loud enough to carry downstairs.

James ignored him and continued to drive at speed around Trafalgar Square while firing a gun out of the window at the trailing police cars.

Alan reached over and thumbed the power off button

on the console. The screen froze and the words GAME OVER scrolled across the screen.

'Idiot.' James pulled off his headphones and dumped them on the console.

Alan dropped into an empty chair. 'I've just delivered your Christmas card.'

'Really? It's not Easter for months.'

'Amy's already said that,' Alan grinned. ', Jayne's coming round to talk about shoes and dresses with Rosie. We had to get out.'

'Fair enough.' James nodded at an empty corner of the room. 'Frankie?'

Alan pointed in the opposite corner. Frankie had made himself comfortable on a pile of books destined for a recycling bank.

James nodded. 'Evening Frankie.'

'Evening big man,' Frankie replied while fidgeting on a copy of *The Davinci Code*.

James passed his friend a beer and a bottle opener from his desk.

'Cheers.' Alan popped the top off and took a sip.

'So, the rubbish dump was a non-starter.'

Alan screwed his face up and shook his head. 'We were never going to find him there. I said it was going to be a waste of time.'

Frankie laughed, receiving a scowl in return.

'So, what's happening then? Are you going to blow out the Hoof's Christmas party and cover Harry?'

Alan took a long pull on his beer and shook his head before putting the bottle down. 'Absolutely not. No way. They're trying to blackmail me, but I'm sticking to my principals.'

'You'll do it,' Frankie said.

Ignoring him, Alan continued. 'Sarah's trying to put it all on me. You know the sort of thing; the agency will fold; Sarah will be homeless, and I'll have to go back to the civil service. That last one scared me, I have to admit.'

James raised his bottle. 'Good for you, mate. You stick to your principals...whatever the cost.'

James,' Amy called out as she walked into the room.

Alan and James exchanged the briefest of looks; An outsider had strayed into their territory. Admittedly, an outsider who was married to one of them, and who part owned the house they were currently in, but an outsider, nonetheless. And in James' den. The outrage! This was James's special place. A place where he practised his guitar (badly), played on his games console (and lost), and marked disappointing homework. It was in this room that he and Alan had investigated the life of Frankie Fortune when he first appeared eighteen months earlier, and now that sanctuary had been breached.

'What?' James snapped.

'The dress. What do you think?' Amy smoothed down the grey, shapeless dress that went down to her ankles.

'Yeah, very nice...very err, bland.' He looked at Alan for help. 'What do you think?'

Alan had hoped Amy had forgotten he was there and frowned. 'Very nice Amy. Are you going out tonight?' Out of the corner of his eye, he saw James shake his head.

'Alan, is this the sort of thing I normally wear?'

'I think...er...no, yes. Possibly?'

Amy sighed and looked at James.

'Amy's taking her class to a living nativity play tomorrow and she's in it,' James explained.

'She is?' Alan asked.

'I'm the Virgin Mary,' Amy told him.

Alan considered several responses before wisely choosing the least controversial option. 'OK.'

Fearing that Alan wasn't positive enough, James added. 'I'm sure it'll be fine.'

Amy frowned and pulled the headdress tighter to her head. 'I think this needs some work, she said and left the room.

Alan sighed. 'Doesn't she know I came here tonight to avoid women talking about dresses?'

'Death by irony,' James said, laughing.

Alan drained his bottle and put it on the desk. 'I'll tell you what, though.'

'What's that?' James asked.

'If she's Mary, does that mean that we're...' He made a circular gesture with his finger, taking in both James and Frankie. 'The three wise men?'

James raised his bottle. 'I'll drink to that.'

'Heaven help us,' Frankie said and put his head in his hands.

FOURTEEN

'...It's only five sleeps to the big day...Come on guys, admit it. You're not ready, are you?'

A hand shot out from under the duvet, banged the top of the bedside table. The hand slapped around on the table-top. No clock radio.

Alan pulled the duvet off his head and forced his eyes open. The bedside table was empty. He pushed himself up on his elbows. He could hear the idiot DJ inanely prattling on about something. Christmas probably. But the sound wasn't coming from where Alan expected. It was quieter, fainter than he was used to. Almost as if it was in another room. Forcing himself out of bed, Alan set off to investigate.

Coming down the stairs, Alan traced the source of the noise to the kitchen. His clock radio was sitting on the kitchen table telling everyone that it saw *Mommy Kissing Santa Claus*. Stuck to the top was a post-it-note. Alan pulled the note away and read the handwritten message.

'Now that you've found your alarm clock, could you turn it off sensibly and not drop it on floor. Love Rosie.

'Bloody cheek,' he grumbled.

'Morning, son,' Frankie strolled into the kitchen. He watched as Alan unplugged the clock and bunched the cable together. 'What's up?'

'Look,' Alan gestured at the table. 'She moved my alarm clock.'

Struggling to contain his disinterest, Frankie shrugged. 'Oh, right.'

'I mean, it's not funny. It's irresponsible. What if I'd overslept?'

'Overslept for what?'

'For...er...I don't know. Something important.'

Frankie pulled a face. 'Of course. All those important things you have to do.'

Any comeback Alan was considering was cut short by his phone pinging. He studied the screen. 'It's a message from Sarah, she says; 'Are you helping us out tonight?'

'Are you?'

Alan put the phone on the counter. 'I'm thinking about it. I'll call her later.'

The phone pinged again.

'She wants an answer now,' He read.

Frankie said nothing.

'Don't look at me like that. I said I'll call her la...' Another ping. 'She's sent me an attachment.'

'What is it?'

Alan tapped the screen and watched as the document opened. 'Oh, very funny.'

'And?'

'It's a list of current vacancies in the civil service.'

Frankie laughed. 'You've got to give her credit. She's playing the game.'

Alan continued to look at his phone. 'She says, *"I hope you find this useful in the new year."'*

'Anything else?'

'Hang on, let me get to the bottom of the page.' Alan glided his finger down the screen. 'Yes, she says, Happy Christmas.'

Another chuckle from Frankie. 'Let me guess, you're going to call her later?'

Alan opened a cupboard. 'First off, I'm going to have my breakfast. Then I'm going to have a shower and then, if I don't have any prior commitments, I'm going to her office and give her a piece of my mind.'

Frankie watched Alan pour cereal into his bowl. 'And then you're going to do Harry's gig, aren't you?'

Alan picked a piece of cereal from the counter and popped it into his mouth. 'Probably.'

'What about him?' Harry leaned over Sarah's shoulder and pointed at a name in her notebook.

'No. Booked elsewhere.'

'Him?'

'Retired. Packed it in last year.'

Harry slumped back in his chair. 'There must be someone who fancies a gig tonight.' He looked up at the ceiling. 'I don't suppose we could persuade Mario to make a comeback?'

Sarah shook her head. Mario was a train driver who spent journeys entertaining passengers on his train with a stand-up (or rather sit down routine). She had persuaded him to do a spot at a comedy club, which was only successful once he sat with his back to the audience. 'Apparently, he's happier making his passengers laugh. He says he gets no abuse or things thrown at him, at least, not because of his jokes.'

'So, it's got to be Alan then?'

Sarah looked at her phone. No missed calls. 'I wouldn't hold your breath.'

'No,' Harry said. 'Alan may be irresponsible and lazy, but deep down, he's a good man. He'll come through.'

Sarah sighed. 'I wish I had your faith.'

There were three raps on the door, and the door opened.

'Morning,' Alan stepped into the room and was met with a beaming grin from Harry and a glare from Sarah.

'Where have you been? I've been trying to call you.'

'Nowhere. I saw your calls while I was coming in,' he lied.

'Why didn't you reply? Let us know you were on your way?'

'It's not safe to make calls when you're driving. You should know that.'

Sarah frowned. 'You don't drive here. You get the bus.'

'Yes, but I didn't know that you weren't driving.'

Sarah shook her head. 'So, tonight.'

'About that, I...' Alan paused, his phone vibrated in his pocket. 'Hang on,' he pulled his phone out. 'It's James... Mate, what's up...He's here, we're at Sarah's...'

He offered his phone to Harry. 'He wants to speak to you. Says you're not answering your phone.'

Harry took the phone. 'Hello James. No, I put it on silent...No, I didn't know you could make them vibrate...'

Alan looked at Sarah and rolled his eyes.

'Really?' Harry said. 'Really...Are you sure? OK then, is she sure?'

Frankie stepped into the office. 'What have I missed?'

He asked, saw Harry talking into the phone and leaned against the wall. 'I can wait.'

Harry said thank you several times and ended the call.

'Who was that?' Alan asked, taking his phone back.

Harry frowned. 'That was James...'

'Really?' Alan said sarcastically. 'Who would have guessed?'

'Anyway, as I said, that was James. He said Amy called him, and she said...' Harry paused for a moment and pulled a face that seemed to suggest he was having trouble processing the information that had just been shared with him.

Ignoring Alan, Sarah asked. 'And what did she say?'

'That she might have found Ernie.'

Frankie watched in silence as they considered Harry's news. Eventually, Sarah asked. 'Is she sure?'

Alan said. 'Where?'

Sarah said. 'Where did she find him?'

Alan said. 'Is she sure it's him?'

'Did James say where she saw him?' Sarah asked.

'No. He just said Amy thinks she's found Ernie and I should call her.'

Alan handed his phone back. 'Go on, then.'

'Don't get your hopes up just yet,' Sarah cautioned.

Harry put his hand up. 'It's ringing...hang on...Hi Amy...no it's Harry...No, I don't know why I'm using Alan's phone. He just gave it to me...OK, yes, James said you had found Ernie...OK, yes, see you later.'

'And?' Alan asked.

'She said it's a bit tricky to explain on the phone and could we meet her at The Vicarage Tearooms in thirty minutes?'

'Where's that?' Alan asked.

'Amy said she would text you the address,' Harry said, passing the phone back to Alan.

Sarah stood up. 'Come on then. Let's get going. Harry, you may still get to do your gig tonight. And Alan, there's still a chance you can get to your grotty pub.'

Frankie shook his head as he watched Alan and Harry eagerly follow Sarah out of the office. If he had learnt anything over the last eighteen months, it was that whenever Alan and his friends got involved in anything; it was never straightforward.

FIFTEEN

The Vicarage Tea Rooms sat at the bottom of Leppers Hill. Formerly a fully functioning vicarage occupied by the local parish vicar, his family and housekeeper. It had been sold in the late eighties when orthodox religion was replaced by the new religions – money, wealth, and power. Converted to a café, it sold hot drinks and light lunches. Usually with a clerical theme.

'That's James's car,' Harry pointed out as Sarah drove into the car park.

She steered her Corsa into the vacant bay alongside the Pink SUV. The car had barely come to a halt before Alan had opened the door and was outside, stretching.

'I can't believe it's taken us forty-five minutes to drive here. It would have been quicker to walk.'

'That's Christmas shopping traffic for you,' Harry said.

'Another reason I don't like Christmas,' Alan complained. 'It always happens when the shops are busy.'

Frankie, who had been sitting in the back alongside Harry, stared up the hill at the church and shivered. 'I don't like churches. It's like they know I shouldn't be here. We're like two magnets pushing each other way.'

Frankie turned to Alan, who was halfway across the car park talking to Harry and had not heard a word he had said. Frankie took another look at the church and hurried after them.

The tea rooms were busy with Christmas shoppers taking a break from the shops and crowds. James and Amy had secured a corner table. Amy waved when she saw Alan come through the doors.

'Morning,' Alan said. 'Actually, it might be afternoon. Whatever.'

James nodded. 'Mate.'

Alan slipped into the chair opposite James while Harry pulled out a chair for Sarah before sitting down himself. 'OK Amy. We're here. Have you found him?' He asked hopefully.

Amy put her cup down. 'Well...'

'Sorry,' Alan interrupted and stood up. 'Hold everything. I need to get something from the café. I haven't eaten for ages...'

'About two hours,' Sarah added.

'Anyone want anything?' Alan offered.

Armed with an order of coffees, teas, and something chewy with raisins for James, Alan stood in front of the counter and waited while the waitress listed the choices.

'Christmas spiced buns, spiced Christmas buns, mince pies, Christmas pudding, Panettone, Yule Log, Christmas cake, Twelfth Night Christmas cake or Christmas Cookies.'

'What's Twelfth Night Christmas cake?'

'Christmas cake without icing.'

Alan frowned. 'What?'

'The snow's melted.'

Alan nodded. 'Very good.'

'Do you want a slice?'

'Any crisps?'

'Only Roast Turkey flavour.'

Alan sighed. 'A slice of Twelfth Night cake, please.'

'Fruit cake?' James said as Alan put a plate in front of him.

'It's the least Christmas themed thing I could find.'

James nodded, biting into the cake.

Alan passed drinks around the table and slipped the tray under his chair. 'OK, you can tell us now,' he said to Amy.

'Thank you, Alan, that's very kind.'

'No problem,' he said, the sarcasm lost on him.

James mumbled something unintelligible.

'What?' Amy snapped.

James swallowed before saying. 'I said, this cake isn't bad. You should try it.'

Alan reached over, pulling off a large piece and popped it into his mouth, chewing thoughtfully. 'Not bad.'

Harry looked at his two cake eating friends and shook his head.

'Amy, would you mind telling us what you've found? They can catch up later.'

Amy shifted slightly in her seat so she was facing Harry and Sarah. 'I've brought my class to a live nativity at the church up the hill.'

'She's in it,' James said proudly through a mouthful of cake.

'Yes, I'm playing Mary.' Amy glared at her husband. 'Anyway, it starts at three, so I thought I would turn up early, just to go through a quick rehearsal with the others. Long story short, I was sitting in the stable watching the verger getting everything into place and guess what was in the manger?'

'Baby Jesus?' Alan said.

Amy produced her phone from her coat pocket and swiped the screen. Without saying a word, she passed it to Harry.

A smile spread across Harry's face.

'What is it?' Alan asked. 'Show me?'

Harry passed the phone to Alan, who studied the screen and frowned. 'I did not expect that.'

James looked over Alan's shoulder. 'Can I?' He asked and took the phone. He moved his fingers across the screen and shook his head. 'Blimey.'

'And?' Sarah asked.

'You're not going to believe this,' James said.

'What?' Sarah snapped.

'Baby Jesus looks exactly like Old Man Ernie.'

SIXTEEN

EARLIER THAT DAY

The Reverend Septimus Maximus III of the Church of The Eternally Nervous Altar Boys stared at his reflection in the hallway mirror. He adjusted his dog collar, ran his fingers over his balding head, and sighed. It wasn't perfect, but it would do.

Septimus had long since accepted male pattern baldness. It was one of several annoying traits inherited from his father, the Revered Septimus Maximus II. But, as annoying as those traits were, nothing irked him as much as his name. Though this was more the fault of his grandfather; Septimus Maximus, who added 'I' to his name when his own son was born. Instead of sounding reverential, he sounded like a Roman soldier. Or a Transformer.

Bullied at Sunday School for both his name and his early onset pattern baldness, Septimus formed a love/hate relationship with his religion. He loved his God, but hated people. Especially those from his own Church. Some of his parishioners weren't so bad. Mainly because they asked nothing of him. But there were others, so many others, who seemed to require divine guidance for irrelevant nonsense such as choosing which sausages to buy from the supermarket. It was exhausting.

Still, he never let his dislike of people distract him from doing good. The fact he often earned a few quid along the way was merely a bonus.

Septimus took one last look into the mirror, before closing his eyes and offering a quick prayer to a picture of his preferred deity hanging on his wall.

'Dear Lord, our Holy Father, thank you for this day. I pray I will act with kindness and according to your wishes. Love and peace. Amen.' He opened one eye. 'And please let my accumulator come in at the 3.15 at Haydock Park. There's a new Mandalorian figurine Daddy needs to complete his collection. Amen,' he repeated. Somewhat as an afterthought.

Satisfied he had fulfilled his duty, Septimus nodded at the picture of George Lucas. He bent and kissed his Chewbacca plush toy for good luck, picked up his small backpack and began his day.

An icy breeze greeted Septimus as he opened his front door. 'For God's sake,' he muttered and went back inside to retrieve his Star Wars beanie hat from the hallway table and pulled it onto his head. He took a quick look in the mirror. Satisfied, he closed his front door and set off at a brisk pace toward the church.

Septimus was keen to get a head start on things today. He ran through his thoughts for Sunday's sermon. Each week he would link a Bible story with a scene from the Star Wars franchise. This week's homily centred on looking after one another and being vigilant against the Devil's machinations. Septimus considered the Star Wars scene where Obi Wan Kenobi tells the stormtroopers *"these aren't the droids you're looking for,"* was the most appropriate.

He was especially keen to make the sermon as short as possible as he had plans to watch the Exorcist on Sunday. It was always good to do some homework. He had bought cheese and crackers to eat during the film, and an expensive bottle of Port. The latter given to him by a grateful parishioner who had to be reassured he hadn't seen a likeness of the Devil in his toast. Darth Vader, perhaps. But certainly not Satan.

A vibration in his trouser pocket alerted Septimus to the fact someone was calling him. He fished around in his pocket and pulled out his phone, swiped the green button and answered.

'Hello, yes?'

'Septimus? It's your mum.'

Septimus sighed. The last thing he needed was a sermon from his mother.

'I haven't heard from you in weeks, so I thought I'd call to see how you are.'

'I'm fine, mum.'

'Are you sure? You don't sound fine.'

'Honestly, I'm fine.'

'Well, how am I supposed to know that? You never ring. You never visit. Your dad's been worried.'

Septimus knew his father was more interested in horse racing than his son. The one thing, other than faith, that he passed on.

'Look, mum. It's lovely to hear from you but I'm busy writing this week's sermon. Could I call you back later?'

'OK,' his mother seemed reluctant to end the call. *'But try not to talk about the Star Wars this week, there's a good boy. No one wants to hear about Duke Skylander and the space bears.'*

Septimus groaned inwardly, promised his mother he

would call her the moment he was free, then ended the call. He slid his phone back into his pocket and continued on his way.

He had barely walked ten yards before his phone vibrated again. What could his mother possibly want now? He pulled his phone from his pocket and looked at the screen. Val. He smiled.

'Hello, Val. How are you this fine morning?'

'Hello, Reverend. I was wondering if you were already at the church?'

'Not yet. I'm a few minutes away. In fact, I'm just round the corner from your house.'

'Oh, that's perfect. There's a massive spider in my bathroom and I wondered if you could come round and remove it for me? I'm terribly frightened of them and I can't, you know, go...'

Septimus grinned at the vision. 'Isn't Henry there?' Henry being Val's husband.

'No, he's already gone to work.'

'Oh. Of course. I'll be there in a minute. Then perhaps we can go to Church together?'

'Thank you Reverend, that would be lovely. I'll see you in a moment,' she said and hung up.

Septimus reached Val's house and had barely knocked on the front door before Val flung the door open. 'Oh, thank the Lord,' she said. 'Come in, come in. It's this way...' she pointed toward the stairs.

Septimus nodded. He knew the way. He and Val had been in an on-off affair for years, but felt little shame, as Henry was an incorrigible cheater himself. Indeed, it was this that led Val into his arms all those years ago.

'It's in the bath,' Val told him, from the bottom of the stairs.

Septimus opened the bathroom door and peered into the bath. Sure enough, a spider was crawling along the bottom of the bath. 'Jesus,' he leaped back in shock. The spider, if it could even be called that, was almost as big as his fist and appeared to be mocking him.

'Have you got him?' Val called from downstairs.

'Not yet,' Septimus replied. 'I might need a saddle.'

'What?'

'It's OK, I have my Bible, a cross and some Holy Water. I'll exorcise this accursed demon.'

'Don't kill him!'

'I'm more worried about him killing me!'

Septimus took a deep breath and slipped one of his shoes off. He bent over the bath, raising his shoe before bringing it down with a smack on the unfortunate arachnid.

'What's happening?' Val shouted.

Septimus turned his shoe over to reveal a squashed spider all over his sole.

'You haven't killed it, have you?'

'Of course not,' Septimus lied. 'I've trapped it in a box. I'll release it when we get to church. If you don't mind, I'll have a quick pee and we can be on our way.'

Septimus used several sheets of toilet roll to remove the squashed spider from his sole. He dropped the paper into the toilet bowl, slipped his shoe back on and pulled the flush.

'All done,' he said when he reached the bottom of the stairs. Let's be on our way, shall we?'

The unlikely couple set off toward the church, fingers almost, but not quite, touching as they walked side by side.

'Are you all set for the Nativity, Sept...Reverend?'

'Nearly. I'm just missing a baby Jesus, then it's all done.'

'I'm sure we can pick up a doll from somewhere. I'll have a look in the charity shops, or online.'

'Thank you. That would be good. But I don't want you spending too much money.'

Val knew this meant she wouldn't be recompensed by church funds, or by Septimus himself.

Septimus briefly considered offering Val some church funds, but quickly dismissed that idea. Most of it was gambling money and he couldn't win big on the horses if he wasted money on a Tiny Tears doll. Or indeed the church roof.

He was interrupted from his thoughts by a middle-aged man in a flat cap and overalls.

'Morning, Rev,' the man said.

'Morning, Bobby,' Septimus replied.

The man, whose real name was Sam, was known to all who knew him as Bobby Crush, after a famous pianist from the 1970s, whose light-fingered approach to the instrument was not dissimilar to Sam's attitude to other people's property.

'Got some good news, Rev,' Bobby said.

'Oh, yeah?'

'Yep. Just got a delivery of roof slates. Almost new. Only used once. They'd be perfect for your roof.'

'Brilliant,' Septimus beamed. 'May I ask where you got them?'

'Not a good idea, Rev. Let's just say there's a Pentecostal church up the road that might need to do a fundraiser soon.'

Septimus glanced over his shoulder to make sure Val couldn't hear.

'Thanks, Bobby,' he whispered. More loudly, he said, 'The Good Lord thanks you for your kind donation.'

'S'alright, Rev. In any case,' Bobby leaned to whisper in

Septimus's ear 'There's a Methodist church a couple of miles away that will be assisting me to help the Pentecostal church with some new tiles.' Bobby grinned, raised his cap to Val and wandered off in the opposite direction.

'Septimus, what have you done?' Val wheezed.

Septimus burst into laughter. 'I prayed, and God provided.'

Val looked at him sceptically. 'That Bobby is always up to no good.'

'Actually, he is a very big supporter of our church,' Septimus smiled. 'Now, let's hurry, we have a church to get to.'

'Let's never speak of this again,' Val strode purposefully away without looking back.

Val quickened her pace, barely noticing the bin lorry idling in the middle of the road. She did, however, notice what looked like a ventriloquist dummy tied to the front bumper. Funny, she thought. Wasn't it usually teddy bears tied to those vehicles?

She had barely time to consider this before Septimus ran up to her, clutching the ventriloquist dummy. 'Here,' he gasped. 'Stick this up your jumper.'

It was at this point that Val began to consider her life choices.

'You've reached the voicemail of Reverend Septimus Maximus, of the Church of the Eternally Nervous Altar Boys. Servant to the Parish of Merton and loyal servant to God and His son. I'm not available to take your call at the moment. I'm either out doing good or instructing young acolytes on their path towards righteousness. Please leave a message after the tone...'

Sarah ended the call and put her phone on the table. 'He's not picking up.'

'Can't we just go in there and take Ernie?' Alan asked. 'He belongs to Harry, after all. He doesn't belong to the Church.'

James licked his finger and wiped it across the plate, harvesting the last remaining crumbs of the twelfth night cake. 'I've been covering for a history teacher, and I had to take the kids through the reformation.'

'And?' Amy asked.

'The one thing you don't want to do is make the Church angry. They get really, really, pissed off. That's the last thing you want. Especially at Christmas – it's their busy time.'

Alan looked at his friend. 'James, I have no formal qualification in history, but I think the reformation *and* the dissolution of the monasteries involved a little bit more than taking a back a ventriloquist's dummy that didn't belong to them in the first place.'

James shook his head. 'That's exactly what they said about the crusades.'

'I don't think they did,' Harry argued. 'That was more about...'

'Stop!' Sarah hissed. 'All we have to do is speak to this Reverend, explain what's happened and take Ernie home with us.' She put her hand on Harry's shoulder. 'Harry here may have to make a donation to the Church fund, but that's his own fault for not looking after him properly.'

'You make it sound so simple,' Amy said.

'Sarah shrugged. 'Why shouldn't it be?'

Amy gestured at the end of the table where Alan was goading James. 'The reformation...Idiot.'

Sarah shook her head and picked up her phone. 'I'll try him again.' She held the phone to her ear. 'It's still ringing.... It's gone to voicemail again.' She put the phone down.

'What now?' Alan said.

Sarah stood up. 'We go and see him.'

The path leading to the church ran through the middle of a park. Alan and James hung back as Amy led Sarah and Harry toward the church. Even in the chilly December afternoon, a group of teenagers kicked a ball around the hardened ground. Both Alan and James secretly hoping that an errant pass would send the ball in their direction.

When the moment eventually came, Alan pushed James aside, his friend falling to the ground like a barely touched Premiership footballer. Alan stepped on to the grass, preparing (in his mind) a perfectly chipped pass to the feet of the kid facing him.

However, as Alan swung his right foot, his left slipped on the wet grass. The ball struck his right ankle as he fell, flying off to the side as he landed clumsily next to James.

'The English Messi,' James quipped. 'Lucky no one noticed,' he added.

Alan lay on the grass. The damp, uneven, partially frozen ground digging into his back. He looked at the over-cast sky, his embarrassment compounded as Sarah looked down at him and said something he couldn't hear through the laughter.

Even Amy, who Alan was convinced had sold her sense of humour to the Devil for eternal life, was doubled over in hysterics. Just as galling was the laughter from the boys whose ball he had attempted to kick back.

'A little gratitude wouldn't go amiss,' Alan shouted at them.

'You should know better at your age,' Sarah said.

Alan climbed to his feet. 'The grass is wet. If I'd known we were playing a match, I'd have worn football boots.'

'Trust me, mate, football boots wouldn't improve your game,' James replied over his shoulder.

Alan grumbled under his breath while removing grass and half frozen mud from his jeans and followed his friends up the hill.

'If that's the standard of English football, I take it

England haven't won the world cup again?' Frankie grinned.

Alan scowled at him and trudged after his friends.

'Look son,' Frankie said. 'I'm going to bail out here, I think.'

'Why's that? Is it your feet again?'

'Yes, and no. The truth is, I don't feel comfortable near that church. It's like it knows there's something wrong with me.'

'We all think that,' Alan added, somewhat unhelpfully.

'I feel like it's...I don't know, pushing me away somehow.'

'No worries, mate. I don't need you bursting into flames. Can you even burst into flames?'

'I don't want to find out. I'm going to wait by the car,' Frankie said and began a slow walk back down the hill.

Alan shrugged and attempted to catch up with the others.

'The Reverend Septimus Maximum the Third, Church of the Eternally Nervous Altar Boys.' James read from a large sign positioned outside the church. 'That's an interesting name. Have you met him?' He asked Amy.

She shook her head. 'No, but the Verger said he would be back for the service.'

'Right,' Alan said, finally catching up with them. 'Amy, you flutter your eyelashes at the vicar and while he's distracted, we'll go in there and grab Ernie. We'll see you back at the car before you can say *gottle of gear.*'

'No,' Amy replied. 'We'll do what Sarah said. My class is arriving soon, and they expect to see a nativity with real people, real animals and a baby in a manger.' She looked at James, who nodded in support. 'So that's what we're doing.'

Alan rolled his eyes. 'OK. Let's do it your way.'

Sarah stepped back and looked along the church wall. 'Amy, if you can show us where the office is, Harry and I will speak to the vicar.'

The Reverend Septimus Maximus III screwed up the betting slip and threw it toward the wastepaper bin. He let out a deep sigh and picked up the copy of the Racing Post from his desk. Taking a pen, he cast his eye down the list of horses in the following day's races and circled his favourites.

He glanced at the novelty cuckoo clock on the wall and thought he probably had enough time to get to the betting shop and back before he was missed. Not that anyone ever missed him.

Before he could stand up, there were two knocks on the door.

'What now?' He grumbled.

No doubt it was someone wanting something. That was the trouble with this job, there was always someone who wanted something.

Septimus decided the most appropriate response was to pray. The fact this required absolute silence and might mean the person knocking would go away was merely a happy accident. He clasped the small wooden cross hanging around his neck in his two hands, and began, *'Please, God. Let whoever is on the other side of the door go away.'*

Two more knocks caused Septimus to question his faith. He groaned, knowing he had better let them in. The sooner he dealt with them, the sooner he could get to the betting office.

Outside, Sarah knocked twice.

'Maybe he's not in,' Harry suggested.

'We'll just have to wait for h...'

'What?' A voice bellowed from inside.

Sarah glanced at Harry, raising her eyebrows. 'Go on,' Sarah said, nudging Harry forward. He took hold of the handle, pushing the door open.

Harry had not been in a church office since his youngest daughter had been christened. If this room was anything to go by, the standards had slipped considerably. What he saw was an untidy, shabby, dishevelled mess. And that was just the vicar who sat at his equally messy desk and scowled at them.

'Alright, then. What do you want?' The crumpled man asked.

Sarah stepped forward. 'We really are very sorry to disturb you, but we need your help.'

The Reverend Septimus Maximus III exhaled with such force the pages of his Racing Post fluttered before once again falling still.

'OK,' Septimus sighed. 'Seeing as you're here, I may as well take a few details.' He stood and moved round to the front of the desk. He lifted a pile of Bibles from a chair and stood for a moment, scanning the room.

'Now, where did I put it?' Septimus tapped his chin with a finger. 'Ah, here we are...' He picked up a large card-board box smothered in eBay labels, dumped the books in it and closed the flaps.

'Must remember to take this to the post office later...' Septimus paused and lifted a book from the box. 'Can I interest you in one of these?'

'What are they?' Harry asked.

'Signed copies of the Bible.'

Sarah frowned. 'Signed by who?

'Me. Who do you think? The good Lord himself?'

'No thanks,' Sarah said. Harry shook his head in agreement.

Septimus shrugged and placed the book back in the box. 'OK, better get started then. Sit yourselves down.' He nodded at the now book-free chair and pulled another closer to the desk. 'There you go.'

Sarah and Harry stepped around piles of paper on the floor and sat on the chairs offered. Septimus returned to his side of the desk and sat down, pulling a piece of paper from one of the several piles on the shelf behind him.

'Before I take details, I should warn you I've got nothing until next October.'

Harry frowned. 'October?'

'Yeah, I know it sounds a way off but....' He paused, put his elbows on the desk, and leaned forward conspiratorially. 'Look. You seem like a decent couple, so I'll tell you what I'll do...' Harry and Sarah stared blankly at him. 'I can take this off the books. Give me a date and I'll squeeze you in. I can do it for five thousand, five and a half if you want the choir boys. But it'll have to be in cash.'

'I'm sorry Father Maximus,' Sarah said.

'Reverend, please,' Septimus replied.

'Sorry, Reverend. But I...' she glanced at Harry, who shrugged. 'We...have no idea what you're talking about.'

'Aren't you here to book your wedding?'

'No,' Sarah exclaimed - a little too quickly for Harry's liking. 'We're not getting married.'

'You're not?' The disappointment of lost earnings was clear on Septimus' face.

'I am,' Harry piped up.

'You are?'

'To someone else,' Sarah added.

'Next year. In Scotland,' Harry said, proudly.

'And I assume you have someone to perform the service?'

Harry nodded. 'I'm afraid we do.'

'Well, what are you here for then?' Septimus asked abruptly, his patience exhausted now there was no financial gain.

Sarah glanced at Harry. 'Harry here,' Sarah began. 'A couple of days ago, he mislaid his ventriloquist's dummy.'

'You're a ventriloquist?' Septimus asked Harry.

'Kind of,' Harry admitted.

'He's a better comedian,' Sarah added.

'And never the twain shall meet,' Septimus mused.

'No, they do. That's part of his act.'

'Anyway,' Harry picked up the conversation. 'A couple of days ago, after a gig, I inadvertently became separated from my dummy; Old Man Ernie.'

'That's the dummy's name.' Sarah added.

'We looked everywhere. We've spent the last few days walking the streets looking in shops, bins, rubbish dumps. Everywhere we could think of.'

Septimus exaggerated impatient sigh. 'And what has this to do with me?'

'A few hours ago, a friend of ours called me,' Sarah said. 'She was visiting your live nativity, and she saw Old Man Ernie in the manger, wrapped in blankets.

Septimus shrugged. 'I have no idea how he got there,' he lied 'Probably gifted by a parishioner.'

'Well, you see, the thing is, Harry has a gig tonight, and he really needs Old Man Ernie back. Otherwise, we will have to cancel the gig. We stand to lose a lot of money,' Sarah explained.

'We were hoping,' Harry continued. 'That you would let us take Ernie back with us? Obviously, we would make a donation to the church fund...For your trouble.'

Septimus leaned back in his chair; the mention of money piquing his interest. He placed his palms together under his chin as if offering a small prayer. 'I think we can reach an agreement.'

'Excellent,' Harry said, grinning at Sarah.

'Let me think...The Church roof is due to be replaced in the spring and we are still somewhat short of the necessary funds...'

Harry took his wallet out of his pocket. 'I think we could help out there.' He opened the wallet and slipped out two ten-pound notes.

Septimus chewed his lip in thought. 'I think five thousand pounds should do the trick...Cash.'

Harry slipped the notes and wallet back in his pocket. 'That seems an awful lot of money.'

'It's an awfully big hole. Some days it's like trying to deliver a sermon underneath Niagara Falls.'

Sarah leapt to her feet in indignation. 'Put your money away, Harry. I'm sorry Father...'

'Reverend, please.'

'I'm sorry, *Reverend,* but that's ridiculous. Ernie's not worth anything like that.' She glared at Harry. 'Come on Harry, time to go.'

She ushered Harry towards the door.

'I suppose I could let him go for four thousand,' Septimus called after them.

Sarah responded by slamming the door behind her, pulling Harry along by his sleeve and out into the cold air. 'I can't believe that man. What a crook. I should report him to his diocese.'

Harry frowned. 'Do you think he'll take a credit card?'

'You're not paying that man a damn thing.'

'But I really want Ernie back.'

'Oh, you'll get him back. Don't worry about that.'

'And how are we going to do that?'

Sarah turned to face Harry, a look of determination on her face. 'We're going to do exactly what Alan said. 'We're going to steal him.'

EIGHTEEN

Sarah and Harry returned to the Vicarage tearooms where Alan and James were tucking into coffee and cake.

'Where is he then?' James asked, noticing they were without Ernie.

'We have a problem,' Sarah said.

'What kind of problem?' Alan asked, while carefully spooning the froth from his coffee.

'We explained we'd misplaced Ernie a few days ago and that he'd been seen in a nativity play. The Vicar denied any knowledge of where he'd acquired Ernie, so we asked if we could have him back....'

Harry picked up the story. 'I said I was quite happy to make a small donation to the church fund. Unfortunately, there was a massive difference between what we were prepared to pay and what the vicar wanted.'

'How much difference?' Alan asked.

'About five thousand pounds.'

Alan pulled a face. 'Bloody hell, that's extortion,' he exclaimed. 'It's not very Christian, is it? Has he even read the bible?'

'Why so much?' James asked.

Sarah shrugged.

'I told you we should have just taken him from the manger when no one was looking,' Alan said smugly, draining his cup.

'You're right,' Sarah said. 'We should have listened to you.'

Frankie, who had been quietly watching the exchange, laughed. 'And that's not something your audiences say too often.'

Ignoring Frankie's outburst, and James's look of mock surprise, Alan focused his attention on Sarah and Harry. 'So, you're saying we should just rock up to the stable, kick the doors in and swipe Ernie out of his swaddling before Amy turns up with her class?'

'I was thinking we'd be a little more subtle.' Sarah said.

'Subtle?' Alan repeated.

'Well, not as blatant as just taking Ernie in front of everyone.'

'Go on then.'

'We take Ernie back but replace him with another baby Jesus.'

Harry nodded. 'Good plan.'

James put his hand up. 'I have some questions.'

'OK,' Sarah said.

'First.' He placed a finger on the table. 'What do we replace him with? It's not like dummies grow on trees. Second.' Another finger on the table. 'The nativity starts in...' He looked up at the clock. 'Thirty minutes. How will we find another dummy? And third...' He tapped yet another finger on the table, squinting in concentration.'

'What?' Alan asked.

'I've forgotten. I'm sure it'll come to me later.' He

gestured at Sarah. 'Carry on.'

Sarah shook her head. 'Thanks James.'

'Right,' Alan started. 'First things first. We replace Ernie with a real baby. Baby Jesus was, after all, a proper baby.'

'It would be more realistic,' Harry agreed.

'And where exactly do you think we can get a baby from in the next thirty, sorry, twenty-eight minutes? You can't just hire a baby for the afternoon,' Sarah said. 'Trust me, if that were possible, I would have done it long before now to shut my mum up about not having any grandchildren.'

Alan looked between James and Harry, shrugged, and said, 'Come on, people. Look around you. The answer's staring us right in the face.'

'What?' Harry asked, glancing around the tearoom.

'Look closer. This place is full of parents having lunch with their kids...' On queue a baby wailed. 'There you go. I'm sure his parents will be glad to see the back of him for a bit.' He turned back to Harry. 'How much were you prepared to pay for Ernie?'

'Twenty pounds,' Harry told him.

Alan held his hand out. 'Give it here.'

'What are you up to?' Sarah asked suspiciously.

'Relax, I'm going to solve our problems.' Alan stood, took the money from Harry's hand and left the table.

As they watched Alan head towards the crying baby's table, Sarah said. 'Do you think he'll remember to be subtle?'

James shook his head. 'Absolutely not.'

Alan headed purposefully between the tables and towards the couple with the screaming baby.

'What's he doing?' James asked, not interested enough to turn around.

'Well, he's talking to the mother of the screaming kid,'

Harry told them.

'And now?'

'Still talking to the mother...still talking to the mother... still talking to... hold on the father's getting involved now.'

Sarah raised an eyebrow, also without turning around. 'That sounds promising,' she said.

'Still talking,' Harry squinted. 'Now he's coming back.'

James and Sarah turned to see Alan heading back in their direction.

'We've got to go,' Alan said breathlessly, and attempted to pull Sarah up by the collar of her coat. 'Come on.'

'What have you done?' She hissed while shrugging him off.

'Nothing. But they're closing in a minute, and we should be on our way.' Leaving the table, Alan headed towards the exit, giving, Harry noticed, the crying baby's table a very wide berth.

James downed his coffee and stood up. 'Whatever happened, I'm sure it was all a misunderstanding.'

———

'What have you done?' Sarah glared at Alan, who leaned against her car, hands thrust deep into his pockets.

'Nothing. They got the wrong end of the stick, that's all. It was just a little misunderstanding.'

James nodded. 'Told you.'

'What have you done?' Sarah repeated.

Alan shrugged. 'I just asked them if we could borrow their baby for a couple of hours. Told them there was twenty quid in it for them.'

'Seems reasonable,' James replied.

Sarah looked to the sky in desperation and screamed

quietly. 'You're an idiot. You know that don't you?'

Alan opened his mouth to reply but thought better of it.

'You,' she pointed at Alan. 'You stay here. I'm going back in there and I'm going to apologise to the people you've just upset and hopefully that will stop them from calling the police.'

'What about us?' Harry asked.

'You can all stay here. Do not move and do not speak to anyone about anything until I'm back. Do you understand?' Without waiting for an answer, she stormed off back to the tearooms.

Once Alan was sure Sarah was out of earshot, he spoke. 'That's the last time I try to help anyone, ever. Seriously, being helpful is more trouble than it's worth.'

A chill breeze blew past them, and Frankie stepped out from behind the car. 'Sounds like I've missed something.'

Alan reached into his pocket and pulled out his phone. 'It's Rosie,' he lied. 'Probably looking for an update.'

James nodded discreetly. He knew this was Alan's system to speak to Frankie when there were other people around.

Alan gave Frankie a short update, missing the part where Sarah had to apologise to the parents of the baby he had just tried to hire.

Frankie stuck his hands in his pockets and sighed. 'What are you going to do?'

'It's simple, really. We've just got to swap Ernie for a real baby in the next few minutes. Harry can do his gig, and I can get to the Hoof's Christmas party. Everyone's happy.'

'The only catch being, where are you going to get a baby from?'

'I know. Parents can be so stubborn about giving their babies away.'

Frankie laughed. 'Babies always look like Winston Churchill to me.'

Alan's eyes widened as he looked at Frankie. A smile spread across his face.

'Guys,' Alan said. 'I think I have an idea.'

'Right.' Sarah said as she got back to the car park. 'You're banned from the tearooms,' she told Alan. 'But the good news is they won't be calling the police. I explained it was an innocent mistake...Why are you grinning?'

'Because, 'Alan began. 'We've got an idea.'

'Oh really, this will be interesting,' Sarah replied, somewhat sarcastically.

'All babies look like Winston Churchill, right?'

'What? I...suppose so.'

'Do you still have that ventriloquist's dummy that looks like Churchill in the back of your car?'

Sarah pulled her car key out of her bag and blipped the lock. 'I think so.'

Alan stepped round the back of the car and opened the boot. Staring back at him was Winston Churchill. 'We will fight them in the stables,' Alan grinned as he lifted the dummy out.

'You're thinking you can swap that for Ernie without anyone noticing?'

'Why not?'

'I can't believe we didn't think of it sooner,' Harry said.

'It looks more like a baby than Ernie,' James added.

'How do you propose to switch the dummies?' Sarah asked.

Alan chewed his bottom lip. 'We're still working on

that,' he said, looking hopefully at James and Harry. 'Guys?'

'We could set off the fire alarm,' James said. 'When they rush out, we'll go in and do the switch.'

'Is there a fire alarm in the stable?' Sarah asked.

James shrugged. 'I don't know.'

'Wouldn't the stables be the likely area where people would evacuate to in the event of a fire drill?' Sarah asked.

Alan shook his head. 'Idiot.'

'Son,' Frankie said. 'You need to get in there, cause a distraction and do the switch.'

Alan stared blankly at him.

'Get yourself into the nativity.'

'We need to get into the nativity,' Alan said. 'Will Amy let us come in with her class?' he asked James.

'I doubt it. You're not a seven-year-old with special needs,' James told him.

Sarah shook her head. 'Well, he's not seven.'

'Then we have to get in there before she turns up.'

'Or,' Harry said. 'We become part of the nativity.'

Alan and James exchanged looks.

'What do you mean?' Sarah asked.

'There's three of us. Every nativity must have three wise men,' Harry grinned. 'We can be those three wise men.'

'I sincerely doubt that,' Frankie said.

'Sorry Harry,' James said. 'But won't there already be three wise men?'

'Double booking,' Harry told him. 'While everyone is trying to work out who should be there and who shouldn't, Sarah switches Ernie with Churchill and we're done.'

'Sounds like a plan. Of a sort,' Sarah said.

'One thing,' James said.

'What's that?' Harry asked.

'Where are we going to get some frankincense?'

NINETEEN

Sarah paced the car park while Alan and Harry leaned against her car, engrossed in their phones. She sighed and looked at her watch. 'Where is he?' she whined. 'He should have been back by now.'

'He's only been gone ten minutes,' Alan replied without looking up from his phone.

'Yes, but he only went to the petrol station. It's there!' She pointed at the large neon sign opposite the car park gates.

'There's probably a queue,' Harry said and passed his phone to Alan. 'Got it in five.'

Alan frowned. 'That's not possible,' he said. 'There must be a glitch in the game,' He added, passing the phone back.

'Shut up, both of you,' Sarah snapped.

'Here he is, 'Harry pointed at the pink SUV heading towards them. The car swung round and pulled into the vacant space it had occupied less than fifteen minutes earlier.

Alan peered through the passenger side window 'What did you get?' He asked.

'Hang on a minute,' James turned off the engine and opened the driver's door. 'At least let me get out.'

Alan tapped his wrist. 'The meter's running, mate,' he said, following James round to the boot.

'Any Joy?' Sarah asked, as he pulled the boot lid up.

'I got as much as I could. It's a 24-hour petrol station, not a branch of Nativity Items R Us.'

Alan leaned into the boot and pulled at one of the large carrier bags. 'Come on, what did you get?'

James snatched the bag away from him. 'Right, I didn't have much to go on, just your...' he gestured at Sarah. 'Shopping list.' He pulled out a tartan car blanket from the bag and threw it to Alan. 'For you.' Another tartan blanket appeared, 'and for you...'

Harry caught the incoming blanket and held it up. 'What's this for?'

James produced another blanket, wrapping it around his shoulders and letting it fall to his waist. 'These are our robes.'

Sarah pulled a face. 'What?'

James sighed. 'You said to me, no more than ten minutes ago, to go into the petrol station and see if I could get some towels. Or anything we could use to disguise ourselves as the wise men from the nativity.'

'Yes, but these are blankets.'

'Because they had no towels. These are the next best thing.'

'He's got a point,' Alan said, having wrapped himself in the blanket and pulled it up under his chin.

Harry, who was nursing his blanket in his arms, said, 'it's not very regal, is it? It's just us wrapped in blankets.'

James grinned. 'I thought of that. Look what else I got.' He reached into a smaller carrier bag and produced three pairs of garishly coloured children's plastic sunglasses. He passed a pair to Alan and Harry before slipping on the last pair. 'What do you think?'

Alan squeezed his glasses over the bridge of his nose with his finger and nodded. 'Oh yes, I like this.' He looked at his reflection in the rear passenger window of James's car. 'Nice. I think we're going to pull this off.'

James and Harry joined him, admiring their reflections in the window. All three of them nodding in approval.

Frankie stepped behind them and shook his head. 'Three wise men indeed.'

'James,' Sarah said.

James prised his sunglasses from his face. 'What's that?'

'Tell me. What part of the nativity involves a three-piece Peruvian pipe band?'

He raised his hands. 'Use your imagination. If we act like wise men, they'll think we're wise men. Anyway, this isn't all I got.'

'It isn't?' Sarah groaned inwardly.

'No. I remembered to get the gifts that the wise men took.' He pulled another carrier bag from the boot. 'Gold,' he announced, pulling out a string bag of chocolate coins wrapped in gold foil. These he passed to Alan.

'Thanks mate.'

'Frankincense,' James produced a car air freshener shaped like an apple.

Harry sniffed it and coughed.

'And for me, myrrh.'

'What is myrrh?' Alan asked.

James shrugged. 'I don't know. I got a carton of long-life milk instead.'

'Why?'

'It begins with an M.'

'Fair enough. No one knows what myrrh is anyway,' Alan said. 'Anything else?'

James shut the boot. 'No. That's it. Do you think I needed to get more?'

Sarah shook her head at the three men huddled in blankets and wearing sunglasses Sir Elton John would have avoided as being too eccentric. 'No, James. I think you should stick with what you have.'

'OK,' James adjusted his blanket.

Frankie looked over at the stables. 'Son, I think you should get a move on. Looks like the show's about to start.'

Alan watched a queue of school children form at the stable. 'I think we should go now,' he repeated.

'I think we'd look more realistic if we arrived on camels,' James said.

Frankie shook his head. 'I think you'd look more realistic if you didn't bother.'

Sarah sat the Winston Churchill doll on the roof of her car and locked the doors. 'We don't really have much of a plan, do we?'

Harry frowned and looked at Alan, who shrugged. 'We'll improvise and wait for the right moment to get it done.'

Sarah dropped Churchill into a bag and followed the others across the car park.

An orderly queue of school children filed into the car park in pairs. Alan, James, and Harry joined the back of the queue, trying and failing to look inconspicuous. A teacher at the rear of the queue turned to them. 'It's not fancy dress, is it?'

Alan laughed. 'No, we're the three wise men. We're running a bit late.'

'We took a wrong turn at the sea of Galilee,' James explained.

'Idiot,' Alan said under his breath.

'Anyway, you should probably jump the queue...'

'Before there's no room at the Inn,' James added.

Harry shook his head and led them to the front of the queue.

Sarah muttered a string of apologies as they squeezed past the queueing school children, through the wooden door and into the stable. She slipped to the side as they entered the stable and took in the scene. Several children sat on the floor and, as more entered, a teacher directed them to sit down facing the front.

Three donkeys formed a semi-circle around a manger and a small wooden stool, tethered to a couple of posts which appeared to be supporting the ceiling.

Sarah suspected Ernie was already in the manger. She assumed the realistic element of the nativity allowed for live animals but perhaps not Amy, dressed as Mary, giving birth.

Sarah considered an attempt to switch the dummies now, before anyone noticed. It would certainly save a lot of bother. As she debated the pros and cons, the doors to the other end of the stable opened. A man dressed as Joseph and Amy dressed as Mary walked in, taking their places around the manger. They were followed by an Inn Keeper. Then, more significantly, three realistically dressed wise men wearing white robes, small crowns and carrying staffs.

'They're wearing the home kit,' James whispered to Alan.

'Time to up our game,' Alan whispered in return, stepping forward. 'Who are you supposed to be?' He called out.

The wise man nearest to them pointed at his chest and mouthed *us?*

Alan nodded. 'Yes.'

'We're the three wise men,' the wise man said.

Alan shook his head. 'Sorry. I think you'll find we're the three wise men.' He gestured at James and Harry standing on either side of him.

'Don't be ridiculous,' the wise man said. 'We were asked to be the wise...' He paused. 'And look at you, you look like.... blind wombles.'

It was at this point all six wise men realised that everyone, adults, children, even the donkeys, had stopped what they were doing to watch the scene unfold.

'Go on, son,' Frankie grinned. 'You've gone past the point of no return now.'

'That's blindist,' James said as a teacher laughed.

'I think we must have been double booked,' the wise man said.

'We have come bearing gifts for the newborn king,' Alan announced, thrusting his petrol station carrier bag at the man.

Harry nudged Sarah, nodding at the manger.

While this scene was playing out, Amy, who had taken her position on the stool, stared open mouthed. 'James!' She called out in horror.

James pushed his sunglasses further up his nose and tried to hide behind Alan.

'We have also come bearing gifts,' the wise man said and held out a neatly wrapped gold present.

Alan, James, and Harry took a step toward Amy and the manger, a move mimicked by the real wise men.

'You should go,' the wise man said. 'It's time for the professionals.' He laid his gift in front of the manger.

Amy sat on the stool, her head pounding, expecting at any moment a bolt of lightning to hit the stable, when Sarah appeared at her side.

'Hello,' Sarah mouthed and produced what looked like a Winston Churchill doll from a bag.

Amy opened her mouth to speak, but before she could say anything, Alan dropped a carrier bag at her feet.

'Too late. I've baggsied it,' he said.

'Nice one, mate,' James said.

'You can't do that,' the wise man said.

Frankie, who had, until now, been enjoying the spectacle play out from a position at the back of the room, moved in for a closer look. He slipped behind Joseph and leaned against a post. 'This is great,' he whispered to the nearest donkey, who looked up in surprise from chewing on a bale of hay.

Frankie instantly realised his mistake. He wasn't sure if animals could see him, or just sensed his presence, but they invariably reacted to him noisily, and sometimes aggressively.

'Oh, sh...' he shrieked, as the donkey brayed in response, lurching toward him.

The entire stable turned as one to see a panicked donkey straining to get across the stable, as it brayed and pulled at its leash Frankie disappeared.

Instead of placating the startled animal, Frankie's disappearance seemed to agitate it further. The donkey reared up on its hind legs, straining against its tether, dislodging the post.

What occurred next appeared to Alan to happen in slow motion. The startled animal pulled harder at its leash, snapping the post in two. For a split second, the two pieces of wood remained motionless before the roof collapsed, causing a billowing explosion of hay and dust to shoot into the air.

The kids roared with laughter, thinking it was part of the nativity. Joseph tried to calm the agitated donkey, while Amy was torn between beating her husband to death with the manger or leading the children to safety. Sensibly, she chose the latter. Harry helped the Inn Keeper to his feet while James slipped outside to avoid his wife.

While chaos ensued, Sarah lifted Ernie out of the manger and replaced him with Winston Churchill. She tucked Ernie under her coat and calmly walked out of the stable.

Their blankets and sunglasses safely stowed away in James's boot, Alan, James, and Harry sat in the car and waited for the fuss to die down.

'The ambulance is leaving now,' James said, looking in the rear-view mirror.

'That was a massive overreaction,' Alan said. 'No one got hurt. And I guarantee those kids had a better time than they would have done otherwise.'

'The fire engine is leaving now,' James told them.

'That was a massive overreaction,' Alan said. 'No one got trapped under anything or needed cutting out.'

James looked again in the rear-view mirror. 'The police are leaving now.'

'That's why we're staying in the car,' Alan said. 'Just in case they feel the need to blame someone.'

The passenger door opened, and Sarah climbed into the car. 'OK, so that's over.'

'I take it no one is looking for us?' Harry asked.

Sarah shook her head. 'No. But the police want to talk to the vicar about hosting a nativity in an unsafe building.'

'So,' James said. 'We're in the clear.'

Sarah laughed. 'Actually, one of the proper wise men said if you lot weren't there, one of them could have been standing under the roof when it collapsed. So yes, you're in the clear.'

'Well,' Alan said. 'We're safe, mate. But you've still got to face Amy.'

James sighed and looked out of the window. 'Shit.'

'Still,' Sarah smiled. 'We've got Ernie, so Harry can do the gig tonight and Alan, you and James can go to that grotty pub for its Christmas party.'

Alan leaned back in his seat. 'And just for once, everything turned out OK.'

TWENTY

Alan and Frankie stepped from the bus into the swirling snow, passing drunken revellers as they made their way to The Cloven Hoof.

'It's funny,' Frankie said, as a woman dressed as an elf staggered past him. 'All these people are walking away from the very place you've been so desperate to get to all week.'

'Your point being?'

'Maybe it's not the big draw you seem to think it is.'

'Trust me. It's going to be a great night. Nowhere does Christmas like Gary in the Hoof.'

Frankie nodded, unconvinced as they passed a man wearing a Santa hat relieving himself against a wall. The man called out; 'Happy Christmas,' over the sound of splashing.

Alan stepped over the stream. 'You too, mate,' he said as they turned onto the road where The Cloven Hoof was situated.

'Looks like Gary has made an effort,' Frankie pointed ahead. 'That's a decent set of Christmas lights.'

Alan saw several blue lights flashing in unison.

'They're a bit of an upgrade from your usual set of lights from Woolworths,' Frankie added.

Alan laughed. 'It's about time I brought you up to date on a few things.'

As they drew closer, it became apparent the lights were coming from the road rather than the pub itself.

'I've got a bad feeling about this,' Alan quickened his stride.

'There's James,' Frankie said, while trying to keep pace with Alan.

James, head down, hands in his pockets, looked despondent. A strip of police tape stretched across the pavement, prevented access to the pub. The source of the impressive lights now revealed as the lights from a police van and two police cars parked across the road.

'What's going on?' Alan asked.

'I don't know,' James said. 'It's been like this since I got here. They won't let me in.'

'It's definitely trouble at the Hoof?'

James nodded.

Alan ducked under the tape only to be confronted by a police officer stepping out from the pub.

'Can I help you, sir?' the officer asked in a tone that suggested he had no intention of helping anyone.

Alan stepped backwards and under the tape. 'Officer,' Alan said. 'My friends and I were wondering how long before we're allowed to go in...' He nodded at the pub entrance.

'Not for a while, sir.'

'An hour?' Alan asked. 'That's OK. We can wait.'

James nodded. 'An hour is fine.'

The officer smiled, but it didn't reach his eyes. 'No sir. It won't be an hour. To be honest, I don't know when this place will be open again...' He looked over his shoulder and lowered his voice. 'It appears the landlord has got himself into a spot of bother with Customs and Excise.'

'Really?'

'He's been selling dodgy bottles of vodka.'

'Has he?' Alan asked innocently.

'Perhaps you might know something about it? What with you and your friend here being regulars?'

'No,' Alan snapped back. 'We're not regulars, are we, James?'

James shook his head. 'Never been in here in our lives... ever.'

The officer stared at them. 'It's just you seemed eager to gain entrance. I assumed you were regulars.'

'No, no. Not all.' Alan put his hand on James's shoulder and began moving him away. 'We'll be off then. Merry Christmas, officer.'

'Merry Christmas, sir.' The officer watched Alan and James march back down the road, shook his head, and went back into the pub.

'What are going to do now?' James moaned. 'It's bloody typical of Gary to ruin my night out.'

Frankie tapped Alan on the shoulder. Something Alan still could not fully understand. 'So, I guess you two need somewhere else to go? Somewhere with a late licence?'

'That's about right,' Alan told him. 'Do you have anywhere in mi...Ah.'

'What?' James said.

'I suppose,' Alan began. 'That it was inevitable.' He sighed. 'Bugger.'

'What?' James said again.

'If we get a move on, we'll be in time for Harry's gig.'

HAPPY CHRISTMAS

EPILOGUE

Three Weeks Later.

'Good morning sleepyheads. Come on, wake up and get up. Let's start the new year as we mean to go on.'

A hand emerged from under the duvet, feeling around on the bedside table for the clock radio.

'...and it's certainly a good start for the employees of The Shining Beacon Community Recycling and Waste Collection Centre...'

Alan stopped and pulled the duvet off his head.

'...It turns out that a candlestick they rescued from landfill is one of a pair of rare Chislet candlesticks which has been missing for over one hundred years. It goes up for auction in the new year and is expected to fetch half a million pounds....'

Alan swiped the radio off the bedside table and went back to sleep.

Printed in Great Britain
by Amazon

35296580R00094